TIRZAH M.M. HAWKINS

His Game

The First Time and The Woods

Contents

I

His Game: The First Time

Rachel's your average teenage girl, fresh out of high school, excited about the secret trip her boyfriend surprised her with. She's been waiting forever for him to pop the question.
However, John isn't your average teenage boy. And his idea of a fun trip is far from a proposal.
John's growing into his tastes. Tastes for things unmentionable in polite society. Read this coming-of-age story about how a violent artist got his start.

1

The Dark Web

As I watched Rachel in the icy water, sinking below the surface, and bobbing up gasping for breath, I knew I wasn't a murderer. Of all the other things I was turning out to be, I would hold that distinction and protect it with my integrity.

Leading up to the day of the event, I didn't plan or premeditate the attack. Not beyond my girlfriend's face mixing in with others in my frequent violent fantasies.

Daylight hours pass for me in a long, dull boredom. But when I lay down and close my eyes at night, my imagination transports me to exciting places. Behind the safety of my eyelids, I visualize scenes I can't speak of to anyone. Lovely, horrible, savage, bloody, shocking things.

They were always meant to be just that: dreams. Secret fancies of a being with tastes unmentionable in polite society. Things I can never mention to my mother nor allow her to know I watch. Her PTA groups, Bible study cronies, and red hat loonies would clutch their chests and faint after less than a minute of my ideal form of entertainment.

In fact, the only person who comes close to knowing how deep I've plunged is my buddy, Zach. Yet, even he doesn't know the full extent of it.

It all started the last week of high school. Zach and I were walking home together...

* * *

"Want to explore the dark web with me?" Zach asks with all the coolness of someone offering me a drink of ice water on a hot summer day. He looks at me out of the corner of his eye and grins.

I answer like a man who's been lost in the desert and on the verge of death. "Heck, yes. You'd better not be bluffing, man."

"Don't worry. I couldn't be more serious."

"I'm going to call your bluff. You've been talking about getting us on the dark web since sophomore year."

"Calm your tits, Johnny boy. I discovered the secret."

If he'd dangled anything less appealing in front of me, I would've decked him. As my best friend, he knows I hate being called that. Not that it's much better than plain John, named after my mother's favorite apostle. Something about him being the closest to Christ or some shit.

"If you value your tongue at all, you'll hurry up and tell me, dude."

He swivels his head like a paranoid asshole.

"No one's around. Come on!."

As we walk down the suburban sidewalk on this sunny June day, the nearest person is old Mr. Parkinson out mowing his lawn. As usual. He's out there most days like a boring adult with nothing better to do.

Mr. Parkinson notices us and raises his hand. We wave in return, willing to pretend like we belong here. I think Zach longs to get away and do something exciting with his life as much as I do.

Zach continues in a low voice. "I was hanging out with Nate's oldest brother, and he showed me the trick."

Maybe my friend isn't lying to me. Nate's oldest brother is known as one of the best hackers around.

"No, shit." My heart pounds in my chest with a fervent giddiness.

"Yes, shit. I had to promise to do some work for him as payment. But the videos I watched last night, fucking incredible." Zach turns up his face and folds his hands like a devout man in prayer.

I elbow him hard enough for him to rub his ribs and walk straight again. "Why didn't you tell me?"

"Bro, I was jacking off so often I couldn't think. After four or five, I kind of stumbled into bed and passed out."

"What things were you watching?"

My cock pulses in my pants. I know Zach better than to think something lame like titty pics made him this excited. We both drool over the fleshy bondage magazines. Especially when the women wear a pained expression. Now that's art. The kind I'd like to create.

"Beyond words, my man. Just wait."

A silent agreement passes between us, and we pick up the pace to something I imagine resembles the local mall walkers. When I was younger, my mom wanted to join them for exercise. I sat on a bench in the middle of the aisle, unwilling to be seen chasing around those old farts.

I pant with anticipation now. We can't reach Zach's house

fast enough.

His mom greets us as we dash inside and quick-step it to the stairs. "Hi, boys. Do you need a snack?"

"Maybe later, mom."

I nearly walk on his heels as we scamper up to his room and close and lock the door.

Zach plops down into the chair in front of his computer while I stand behind him. The sound of our gasping breaths is the only thing louder than the pounding in my temples. The last time I recall being this excited was the Christmas before realizing Santa Claus wasn't real. Discovering the dark web is a lot more exciting than any lame holiday.

"All right, my man, are you ready for this?" He punches keys like crazy. The monitor changes from the bright, cheerful, elementary colors of Google to a black screen with white text.

All moisture vacates my mouth. After this, we'll never go back. The normal person's internet will hold no interest for us. The world of nightmares and dreams is now open for our pleasure and participation.

"What do you want to see first?" Zach stops and turns to look at me.

I'm torn for a minute between what I want and what I think my friend can handle. How closely do our tastes align? Does he lie awake at night wishing to hear women scream and beg for their lives?

I decide to go for it. Why not? If he balks, I can laugh and pretend it was a joke.

"I want to watch someone die."

Zach stares at me, unmoving. Only his eyes twitch back and forth as he studies me.

I wait for something more, some sign I crossed a line. But it isn't there. He's not adamantly telling me that our fetishes are worlds apart. That's when I realize he's interested, too.

"Got it." He rotates back to put his hands on the keyboard. "Be prepared for your mind to be blown."

* * *

His warning was useless. Nothing could have equipped me for what Zach showed me.

The video doesn't last long, maybe ten minutes. By the end, both of us sport massive tents. I'm surprised neither of us jizzed from what we'd just watched.

"I'll be in the bathroom." The words haven't fully left my mouth when I bolt for the door. From the corner of my eye, I see him fumbling with his jeans.

"Right," he mumbles.

I can't get out of the room fast enough. My cock throbs with need more painfully than ever before. My most realistic wet dreams don't come close to the beautiful, amazing agony we witnessed.

I lock the upstairs' bathroom door and free my erection. The first stroke is sweet ecstasy as I replay everything in as much detail as I can remember.

The camera closes in on the woman's face as someone pulls a cloth off her head. Her wide eyes dart about like a frightened wild animal. With the gag in her mouth, all her words are muffled and useless. That doesn't stop her from trying. The incoherent cries and pleas sound real enough to me.

The shot pans out, revealing a dark room. Hooks and chains line one of the walls. I'm envious of their setup and how realistic it looks.

Whips and canes hang on nearby racks, implements of a true artist. I want to know what screams each one evokes.

As the scene widens, I see a man with a blurred face standing next to the woman. He caresses her bare skin.

With slight disappointment, I realize we're catching the second half of this act. The woman's white flesh is already marred with lacerations and bruises. I'm more interested in how those came about than the fact that the man is bending her over a waist-high, rounded, wooden stand.

She squirms and wiggles her shoulders, trying to free her hands which are restrained behind her back. Her tired moans turn to shrieks as she realizes what's happening.

The man steps behind her and thrusts inside her pussy. The camera turns to give us a view of the penetration.

My eyes hone in on the marks on her body, the trickle of blood from her tied wrists. The signs of torture are more exciting to me than the rape.

The scrapes. The raised bruises. The dripping cuts.

While the man pounds into her, I imagine the sounds she made as she received those wounds. Each type of anguish must have elicited a different noise. Blunt trauma versus sharp, cutting blades. Gagged in comparison to an open mouth. This is what I need more of. The exploration of human pain. With all of it ending in finality.

As the man nears orgasm, he grabs a length of rope and wraps it around her throat. The camera closes in, first capturing the penetration with the beginnings of the strangulation. Then it hones in on the woman as she struggles for air. Her eyes bulge like they might pop from her face.

I quicken my strokes, my body jerking with the nearness of my finish as the life drains from the woman on the screen in my memory. I turn and point my dick into the shower as my come bursts from me. The climax is like nothing before. My imagination had been unable to create an image so delicious.

After today, my life will never be the same. I've opened a box I cannot, nor want to, close.

I watch my thick white fluid drip down the sides of the tub as my cock does a final spasm or two in my hand and decide to leave it. I don't care. All that matters to me now is my next fix. I must have more.

No. More isn't nearly enough. Beyond a shadow of a doubt, I will never be satisfied until I'm producing my own shows.

Zach said earlier that the best stuff was locked behind a paywall. How much better can it get? How many people are out there waiting for my art?

I tuck my dick into my pants as I remember my favorite part of it all. The shot never broke, never cut away as they choked the lady. The audience was allowed to watch her lifeless body fall to the ground. The man who fucked her placed a small mirror by her nose.

The video timer ticked, marking the passing of seconds. Zach and I skipped ahead. The producers let it run for five minutes after she fell. Not once did a hint of a fog show on the reflective surface.

We had truly watched someone die.

2

Act One: The Proposal

even months later...

"John. What are you doing?" Rachel pulls her coat around her and swivels her torso from side to side. Her cheeks blush with the cold and something more. Glee? Expectation?

I guess she thinks I'm proposing or something. The idea is a bit preposterous. We're barely out of high school. She was my first kiss and first piece of ass. Nothing special for sure. But she liked to scream when I fucked her.

I envisioned the snuff video I watched with Zach and worse things I saw on my own whenever I was with her. The dark, bloody fantasies in my head made me rock hard. All the better to make Rachel holler. The girl is not a quiet lay.

Which means she'll be loud as soon as we begin, adding to the delightful exquisiteness of the experience.

Planning ahead for her volume, I'd driven us to a secluded park several miles outside a small town. The place is rustic, almost charming under the blanket of snow covering the ground. We stop in a lot near a bridge overlooking the pond.

No one is about. During the summer, people swarm the area to beat the heat. In the middle of winter, it's deserted.

Rumor has it that this body of water is man-made, leftover from a rock quarry. And deep.

Ignoring her, I focus on setting up the camera on the tripod. Not one moment of this endeavor can be missed. I need it all on film. By the evening, I'll be uploading it to a secure server where no authorities will be able to trace it to me. After I blur my body and disguise my voice, no one will ever know who did it.

I lean down and peer through the view-finder taking note of the edges of what it can capture. My only regret is that I don't have anyone to man it, to adjust it if she wanders off. Something to potentially rectify for the future.

When I'm at home later, I can cut it and zoom in and out as desired. I'll edit the shit out of this masterpiece.

My hands shake, not from the chill but from excitement. My cock strains against my pants. No matter. It can wait. This creation is about so much more than mere sexual fervor. Though I'll most likely masturbate to this video more than anything else. All because I discovered my calling. My life's work begins this afternoon.

"John, I'm cold." Rachel bounces on her heels to try to warm herself.

The stupid bitch could've waited in the car. No one told her to get out.

I push my annoyance away. I must stay calm. Be in the moment. Every single amazing one.

"Just another minute. I want this to be perfect." I flash her my best smile, the one that says she means the world to me. The one that hides the fact that she'll be dead in a few hours.

I hope to make it last. Can't blow my wad too early.

As a virgin to this process, I kept the plan simple. Nothing extravagant. Just uncomplicated, everyday tools.

"Okay. I think I got it."

Standing up straight, I note the objects marking the edges of the video without the glass between me and them. The specific fence post on the bridge. The tree on the other side. All the action needs to remain between those two things. We'll start in the middle.

Rachel blows on her hands and rubs them together. "You c-c-could have w-warned me to dress warmer."

"I'm so sorry." I walk to her, allowing some anticipation to show as a smile on my face. "I wasn't thinking." It's winter, bitch. Why didn't you dress for the weather?

I enclose her hands in mine. "In a few minutes you won't be worried about the cold, okay?"

"Yeah. When are you going to tell me what's going on?"

"You'll find out soon enough." Turning away, I run through my mental checklist, almost certain I haven't forgotten any-thing. "Let's start this."

A timer begins on the screen indicating it's recording.

This is it.

I wipe my palms on my jeans. The motion looks natural, I presume.

Rachel giggles. "Come on. I need to know why you dragged me all the way out here."

In response, I lead her out to a spot I selected while looking through the viewfinder.

"Rachel."

"Yeah?" Her breath flows out in a puff from her pouty, pink lips.

I drop to one knee.

She squeals. "Oh my god! You have to be kidding me!" She spins away in embarrassment, covering her mouth, before turning back. "John! Are you serious!"

Fumbling at my shoe like I have to tie my laces, I slip the switchblade out from the bottom of my pants.

My heart pounds in my chest, up my neck, ringing in my ears. Despite the cold, a layer of sweat coats my back. A slight tremble shakes my hands.

This is it: my big moment.

I can't hide the huge grin on my face. Figuring it fits with what Rachel thinks is happening, I look up at her and relish the pure joy shining on her face.

What a surprise this will be.

Time slows.

Not wanting to miss a single reaction, I inwardly groan when I realize I'll need to look away in a minute. For the next few beats, my heart decelerates as I focus on wanting to watch her transformation. Smiling, giggling Rachel now. Terrified, anguished Rachel in only mere moments.

I touch her foot.

Her eyes never leave mine. At no time does she guess that this is about to go horribly wrong for her. Not once does she glance at my arm.

With a quick flick of my wrist, I run the blade across the back of her ankle, slicing into her Achilles tendon as deep as possible. The hour of attention I gave my knife last night proves worthwhile. The edge slips into her flesh, cutting nearly to the bone.

I tear my gaze away from hers for only a fraction of a second, wanting to be sure that the laceration is above the heel of her

Mary Jane's and no higher. Confident in the placement, my eyes meet her again just in time to view the transition.

Nothing has ever brought me so much pleasure.

Bliss melts into confusion. Confusion morphs into pain.

In this slowed reality, her grin becomes a grimace. Her eyes squeeze shut. Her mouth opens. The most amazing shriek of agony and fright issues forth.

I almost nut in my pants.

Rachel grabs her injured ankle, trying to ease the hurt and ebb the flow of the gushing blood. The thick red liquid rushes down and pools around the heel of her shoes.

The sight intoxicates me. I want to stare at the swirling puddle for as long as it moves with the addition from the stream.

A blur of movement flashes in the upper edge of my vision. Rachel tries to run, turning away from me. But her foot fails her, and she falls with a satisfying thud.

I stand up, making sure to not block the view of the camera.

Rachel continues to scream. The sound echoes across the peaceful, snowy landscape. I pray no one is close enough to hear her. Company would be inconvenient.

"What the fuck, John!" She manages a few coherent words as she grapples at the gravel path, trying to pull herself along.

Watching, I enjoy the terror on her face, the whites of her eyes when she opens them wide between winces of pain. For all her efforts, she isn't moving very quickly.

My senses heighten. With hawk vision, I spy the dirt under her nails as she claws at the ground. One of them chips and bleeds with her desperate actions.

Like a part of a play, the first act feels complete. Time for Act Two.

3

Act Two: The Crowbar

With her snail-like, sluggish movements giving me no cause for concern, I saunter back to the still open trunk of the car, and grab the crowbar. The cool weight of it sends a thrill up my arm and down my torso.

My dick twitches. I remind it that this is about more than sex and carnal pleasure. Yes, the orgasm I'll relish later will be the strongest ever, but this is the beginning of something much bigger than myself and my needy penis.

Like a director on a movie set, I'm creating a work of art.

"What the fuck are you doing, John?" Rachel's voice reaches a whole new pitch when she sees me approaching with the iron bar.

Once more, I focus on keeping her in full view of the camera. On my way over, I glance into the viewfinder and adjust it to keep her as the focus.

Her face twists in an ugly, pouting scowl as tears pour down her cheeks. "Why are you doing this? I thought you loved me."

Her words bring me a little pause. She does have a point. In some way, I did love her as my girlfriend. For a time. But that was before I discovered my life's work. Before I witnessed a glimpse of a true piece of art. And isn't that what I want to make? Art?

My soul belongs to a creative. A unique one. A being who needs to operate outside the limits of polite society and produce a rare form of art that only a few kindred spirits will appreciate.

What I'm giving her now is a gift. The chance to be part of something bigger than herself. A muse immortalized. My first love forever captured as my first epic work. While she will never understand, I will never forget her and her sacrifice today.

When I approach with my new weapon, her frantic attempts to scramble away increase in a frenzy. Her gaze darts from the iron, to my face, and back.

"John."

Her pitiful whimpers spur me on.

"Why? What did I do?"

Rachel stills. Either resigned to her fate or not believing that I would hit her. I stop next to her, in clear view of the camera. Raise my arm.

As I strike, I bend my knees to pound her with everything I can muster.

Instinct causes her to tuck into a ball and protect her face and head with her hands. My blow lands on her side, bouncing off a rib.

She shrieks and arches, reaching to cover the wound. A new round of tears flow freely.

On impulse, I crouch on the balls of my feet, wipe a drop from her skin, and lick it from my hand. The salty taste satisfies.

In that instant, I vow to remember this first creation forever. She is setting the stage for a whole host to follow. What painter doesn't remember their first canvas and what they want to do differently the next time? What entertainer doesn't remember their first live concert?

This is the same. My first big show. One I plan to broadcast later this evening if I can concentrate long enough to remove all incriminating evidence.

Not that I'm ashamed. Quite the contrary. A rush of pride warms my veins. My breath leaves my lungs in a puff of cloud; but underneath my clothes, my body sweats.

"Why?" Her questions have reduced to a single whine. Many times over she begs the question.

If I had to reply, what would I say? What possesses me to treat her this way?

Even if I deigned to answer, she would never understand. For the thrill. For the fun. Because I can. Because I need to. Because it excites me.

A flood of new torture devices rushes through my mind. Cattle prods. Tasers. Ropes. Whips. Brands. Needles. Tweezers.

All of this is only a rudimentary list of what's possible. An alternative world opens before me. And I want to document every moment of it. People with refined tastes like mine will pay to see it. And the money I can make will serve to fund future endeavors. Bigger and better setups for inspired filmography.

The world lies at my feet, ready for me to seize.

And seize it, I do. In the form of the crowbar. I lift it again and bring it down. On her upper arm. Her thigh. Her back as she rolls to protect her soft front.

Over and again, I strike, ever aware of where we are in the lens of the camera. Of the way her body jerks and arches in response to every blow. Of the pain that rips from her throat with each scream.

4

Act Three: The Knife

Rachel lies there, bruised, bloodied, and sobbing, seemingly resigned to her fate. Her face is streaked with mascara, tears, and snot.

I stand over her, admiring my work. However, the longer I look, the more disappointed I am. Her thick winter clothing hides most of my efforts. Only her face and hands are visible to show off the fresh discolorations.

I almost wish I had waited until summertime when Rachel would have come out here and shown off her tight little body in a string bikini. Oh, well. I can still make do with what I have. And what I need is more blood.

Whistling a tune, mostly to watch the tiny puffs exit my mouth, I saunter back to the vehicle. I return the crowbar in favor of doing more with my knife.

While my back is turned, I hear Rachel making another effort. Gravel crunches and slides under her.

Where does she think she's going? With one of her ankles out of commission, she'll never escape me.

When I look back, I find her leaning on the railing next to the path, using it as a crutch to help her as she hops along. She's almost out of the view of the camera.

I rush over to head her off, stopping in front of her, blocking her way.

"John." She sniffs, a great strangled noise indicative of the amount of snot clogging up her sinuses.

Her red, swollen face and pleas are pitiful. They do nothing except make me want to continue, to complete my masterpiece. She deserves nothing less after everything she's gone through.

Rachel reaches out to touch my hand. I take hers, relishing the way it trembles in mine. My groin throbs with anticipation. This moment right here will reign supreme in my spank bank for years to come. The way her glossy eyes open wide and plead at me. Like I'll suddenly change my mind and take her to a hospital instead of finishing what I started.

"Please," she whispers.

What a fucking dumbass.

I grip her hand tighter as I throw back my head and laugh. Her expectation is so comical. The best joke ever. It adds a special sprinkle of magic that I couldn't make without her.

"John, please! You're scaring me! I want to go home!" As she continues pleading, her cries increase, making subsequent words unintelligible.

"Shh. It's okay." I pretend to placate her, smoothing the back of her hand with my fingers.

While her eyes are squeezed shut from a sudden fresh burst of tears, I bring the knife up. Turning her wrist to give the recorder a good view, I slice through the veins and tendons below her carpal bones.

A scream bursts from her throat. The loud noise hurts my ears, but it excites me as well. My heart continues a frantic pace.

I want to glance around and see if anyone is nearby. Are her cries summoning people to her aide?

But the camera is watching. I don't want to look like a scared fool. No matter what, I must maintain a brave demeanor and soldier on.

Rachel tries to jerk away from me again. I release her to watch her tumble down against the fence and land with a jolt on her ass.

"Why?" Her tune shifts.

Probably no longer believing she'll get away, she's accepting her fate. The eventuality of her impending demise looms like a shadow over her.

I squat down, grip her hair, and raise the knife to her cheek.

"Because." I dig the tip in, delighted by the way it punctures her puffy skin. "Right now, the two of us are something bigger than we've ever been. We're giving the world a gift. And in death, you will be more beautiful than anyone imagined."

I slice across her cheek, making her scream again. Blood oozes in places and streams in others from the cut. The thick trickling fluid mesmerizes me. I could stare at it for hours if I had the time.

But more work must be done.

I move the knife to the other side. Rachel shrinks back but is stuck in place, prevented from escape by her wounded ankle and the wooden boards behind her.

The second mark satisfies as much as the first. Soon, the veil of blood on each of her cheeks mirrors the other.

What else? What more can I add to this deliciousness in front of me without detracting from what I've already achieved?

I stand up and survey my work, taking it in as a whole.

The curvaceous lobes of her ears call to me. Yes. That will do nicely.

Needing more leverage, I kneel before her again. Once more, I check the angle of the camera. Later, when I'm at my computer, editing, I'll zoom in on what I'm about to do. Make it big so that viewers can notice all the gory, yummy details.

Rachel flinches and makes a pitiful moaning sound when I reach for her again. I grip the tip of her ear with one hand, pulling it away from her head. The sharp knife requires little back-and-forth motion to carve off the flesh.

Rachel flops her good arm in weak efforts to stop me. Her screams now are more subdued and unspirited. She's giving up.

A victorious warmth floods through me.

The end is near. It's approach is bittersweet. How does one complete a work of art such as this? What sort of finale would be suitable?

Allowing myself a moment to think, I walk over to the camera to show off the ear, which looks so small in the palm of my hand.

5

The Finale: Rachel

I stand to the side of the lens, allowing it to focus on the ear while Rachel lingers in the background.

My mind rushes through endless scenarios. I could slit her neck and watch the remainder of blood inside her gush out. I could pound her throat and make her choke on my dick. I could continue to make tiny slices, cut off her clothing, and see whether she bleeds to death or freezes first.

To delay, I step behind the camera and narrow in on Rachel so I can see her wheezing, labored breathing. She holds her injured arm to her chest.

Snot drips down her nose and over her lips. Blood smears her cheeks covering most of the mascara tracks. Enough of the black remains above and peeking below the red to create a perfect, tantalizing picture. I press the shutter button on the recorder to capture the moment in a still version.

Rachel's eyes dart in my direction before looking away to examine her surroundings. She glances over her shoulder, through the boards of the fence.

As if she made up her mind about something, she struggles to her feet.

I wait, wondering what she thinks she's going to do now. In her condition, she won't get far. No one has come to her rescue.

The air is quiet and still, allowing me the joy of hearing her gasping breaths and attempts to clear her nose.

With her good hand, she grabs the fence and uses it to pull herself up. Putting all her weight on her intact ankle and the slat behind her, Rachel glares at me. The weak defiance amuses me. The last remnant of spunk shines through the colors on her face making her look like some insane, angry clown.

"I loved you." Her voice breaks and hitches with each word. "I thought we were going to make a life together.

"And now—," Rachel covers her face as a new sob shakes her. She composes herself and lifts her head once more before continuing. "Now I see you're nothing more than a monster. I hope you die. I hope you rot in hell."

She bends over, leaning in half between the wooden planks.

Confused, I continue to watch, waiting to intercede if she moves close to the edges of what the camera can capture.

She lifts her leg and slides it through the fence, following it with her torso. When she attempts to put weight on her ankle, it gives out. She tumbles sideways and slams down onto the steep slope on the other side with a howling squeal of pain. No more than a second later, she lands with a splash.

I grab the equipment and rush over. The water here is deep, the sides dropping off in a hundred-foot sheer cliff below.

She surfaces and gasps for air.

I stand there, alternating between looking through the viewfinder and not, watching her struggle in the icy lake.

And that is when it hits me.

Rachel *chose* death.

I didn't choose it for her. I hadn't reached that point yet.

In her desperation to escape, she'd rather kill herself than wait for me to finish it.

In this moment, I decide this is how they all will end. No matter how the game starts, I will push them until they lose hope and take their own lives.

6

The Beginning

I spend the rest of the day covering my tracks.

After Rachel succumbs to the frigid water, I fish her out and stuff her pockets and the hood of her jacket with nearby stones to weigh her down. I shove rocks into the waistband of her pants. Once I'm convinced her clothes will hold no more, I roll her back into the deep part and watch her disappear.

Using a tree branch, I swish dirt over her blood. There's less than I imagined there would be and it hides easily.

On my way from the park, I use the limb to brush away all my foot and tire marks, leaving nothing behind.

My hands grip the steering wheel, turning my knuckles white while I drive home. I go in the back door and head straight to the kitchen sink to grab a trash bag. Before walking any further, I strip and shove everything inside.

I bring the bag to my room while I shower.

Once clean, I put on fresh clothes and leave again, storing the bag in the trunk for the rest of the day. Later, I'll burn them. But for now, I drive to Zach's house where I'll play video games all afternoon and evening, creating an alibi.

I had told no one that I would see Rachel today. This morning, I'd surprised her by picking her up unexpectedly. Her parents are out of town. She won't be missed for a while.

When people ask where I was when she disappeared, I was with Zach.

The day drags on as I itch to return home and edit the film.

But I remain patient and engaged. I need my friend to remember hanging out with me all day long.

Finally, it's almost midnight. While muttering about being tired, I make my exit.

Before going about fixing and enhancing the video, I take the time to watch it from the beginning. By the time I'm getting down on one knee, I can't resist my raging erection anymore. I jack off and start it all over. Halfway through, I stroke myself again but wait to finish until Rachel's head pops out from the water.

Yes, I have found my mission in life. Now to share it with others.

Cutting my face, voice, and name out of the film takes longer than I imagined it would. Why did the bitch have to say my name so many times? Spending two days studying the video, I remove all incriminating evidence. Several more pass before I summon the courage to post it online.

I'm certain I've set everything up to be secure and untraceable. Over the last few months, I thoroughly researched foreign bank accounts and money laundering. All from an incognito browser at a coffee shop an hour away.

Finally, one week after the event, I force myself to do it. I put the recording up for people to purchase right before going to bed.

Rather than sleep, I stare at the ceiling. Or the wall. Or the door. Unable to stay in the same position for long. I need to know if anyone will pay me for what I created. Or will all of Rachel's blood, sweat, and tears be for nothing?

Two hours later, a notification dings on my computer.

I jump up and run over.

Success! A rush of pride swells as I struggle to not whoop aloud and wake my mother.

I stare at the three figures sitting in my bank account. My first dollars from this venture.

Only a few minutes later, the mechanical ding announces another purchase. They continue to sound throughout the night like slot machines announcing another jackpot winner. I lie in bed listening with the biggest grin on my face.

Things are only beginning...

7

Author Notes:

I wrote this short story after writing 1.5 seasons of His Game and publishing them on a serial site. After reading season one, my sister Shiloh asked if I would ever write a season from his point of view. That inspired this short story.

I guess that makes this season dedicated to my sister, Shiloh. I wrote it in response to your suggestion, sis.

This one is shorter by far than any of the others, but I hope it isn't any less interesting.

My husband, after telling people what his wife does for a living, likes to remind them that he falls asleep next to my crazy head each night.

I started writing the His Game series after wondering if I could tell you exactly who did it from the first sentence and make you want to keep reading. At no point would you wonder who the monster is. Would anyone still want to finish the story?

Apparently, a lot of people would.

I'm so grateful. These are really fun to write. Don't ask me why. As my best friend Amber said when she read this story, "You are sick."

My favorite form of art is evoking strong emotions in my reader. Happy, sad, love, anger, disgust, horror. I want to capture only the most vivid colors of the rainbow.

When you check out my Ream page, you can sample the first three episodes of every serial story published there for free. ReamStories.com/TirzahMMHawkins.

II

His Game: The Woods

John returns for another game. Only this time he passes himself off as Luke, a former army medic, living alone in the woods with his dog.
Sandra is a romantic. Her idea of a good time is curling up with a love story and her cat. When she's kidnapped, tortured, and left for dead in a forest, Luke looks like the closest thing she's ever seen to a guardian angel.
But the game is still going. And she doesn't realize she's playing.

8

The Tree

Barefoot, she sprints through the woods in just her blood-stained bra and panties. Over her echoing footfalls and pounding heartbeat, she strains her hearing for any indicators of being followed.

Branches snatch and scratch her face and body, but she doesn't slow. She can't slow. If she does, he'll certainly catch her.

Unlike her, *he* hasn't spent the past four weeks recovering from a brutal, savage assault.

How could I be so stupid? How could I have known? Self-contempt and consolation war within her battered mind.

A sudden, stabbing pain sears through her foot, causing her to halt and cry out. She thrusts her hands out to the nearest tree to slow her stumble. In spite of her need for haste, the agony is too much to ignore. She hops on her right foot in order to inspect the bottom of her left, searching for the culprit.

A small branch has impaled the thick flesh of her sole.

Gritting her teeth, she pries it out. The twig sparkles with a sickening sheen. Specks of moss and bark remain in the pulsating wound. Her stomach lurches. She fights against nausea with deep breaths.

Swallowing, she takes a moment to listen. Her surroundings are still. The forest is silent. Most importantly, no footfalls seem to be approaching.

She licks her lips and tastes salt from the sweat pouring down her face.

With her heart hammering in her chest, Sandra squints, scanning the horizon for any sign of civilization. The trees here are rooted so close together that the trunks are lined with only the stubbiest of leafless limbs. Little underbrush fills the spaces in between.

The only sound besides her ragged breaths is a gentle rustling of branches in the canopy. The light fades rapidly now, and she's terrified of being out in the woods by herself after dark. Almost as terrified as she is of him.

Clenching her jaw with determination, she takes off into the mess of trees again, as quickly as her exhausted body will allow.

Less than an hour ago, she had been lying on his bed in her lingerie while he massaged her feet. Recent memories flash through her mind as she races through the forest.

Her insides twist in disgust as she remembers the talented way his strong hands kneaded and stroked away her tension.

When her feet had been properly serviced, he moved up her legs to release the knots in her calves. Then he continued on, bringing his hands up to stroke her thighs. Now and then, he would brush the edge of her panties ever so lightly, making her blush and giggle.

Sandra slows to another unplanned stop and doubles over, clutching her stomach as she struggles not to puke. Bile burns the back of her throat at the surge of recent images. After a few gasping breaths, she presses forward.

Denying her peace, his mocking features continue flashing through her mind.

After massaging her, he laid between her legs and nuzzled her through her panties with his nose. She gasped and arched her back, encouraging him to do more than just tease.

He looked up at her with a sly grin. A stark contrast to the man she'd grown to love. A visage that sent shivers down her spine and erupted her skin with goosebumps.

A flash of color behind him catches her eye. Perfectly placed to draw her attention at this exact moment.

Across the single room of the cabin, on a coat rack near the door, hung a blue ski mask.

The traitorous material stuck out like a disfigurement she couldn't look away from. The placement conveys purposefulness. He left it there for her to discover.

He wanted her to notice it.

As recognition dawned on her, she choked. Icy fingers clutched and restricted her gasping lungs.

Her eyes darted back to him. Beneath his narrow, malicious gaze, a cruel smile lingered on his lips.

"Took you long enough," he taunted. The bed squeaked and creaked in protest as he rose to his knees.

Without thinking, she rammed the heel of her right foot into his chest. Uttering an "oof", he tumbled off backward.

The fall must have knocked the air from him because she managed to rush around him and exit the cabin.

Now, she runs for her life.

* * *

A wolf howls in the near distance.

Her blood freezes. A tear falls and mixes with the sweat on her face.

From behind her, another lupine answers.

Don't panic. Think.

She scans the horizon,searching for the edge of the clearing where the trees will have branches big enough to climb. They can't go on this thickly forever.

Her lungs burn, and her sides ache. After having spent the majority of the last four weeks in bed recovering, she's surprised to have made it this far. The cabin must be a few miles back. Her head swivels left and right seeking for any tree with low branches that can support her weight.

The third howl is closer.

She's being hunted by more than just him.

Please, please, please.

She chokes back the sobs threatening to paralyze her.

Finally, she sees a tree that's worth a try. This is it. She's running out of time.

The limb at shoulder height will hold her if she remains near the trunk. With the help of some stubby, used-to-be branches, she manages to drag herself up onto the offshoot. From there, she climbs another few feet, wanting to put more distance between herself and the predators.

Both kinds.

With her legs straddling a branch, she hugs the weathered trunk and tries to catch her breath.

The single howls echo into a haunting chorus, increasing in volume as the pack narrows in on its prey.

Sandra hitches and sobs in equal parts relief and terror.

Within a minute or two, the bristling animals prowl the

shadows near the base of her tree. Their paws patter over the dried needles on the ground as they circle, seeking the meal they smell but can't find.

The diminishing adrenaline rush leaves her shaking. She presses her face against the rough bark of the fir, inhaling its sweet, refreshing scent, and thanks it for the safety it provides.

Maybe with the sunrise, the wolves will retreat to wherever wolves go during the day, and she'll be safe to move on.

To comfort herself, she imagines her rescue. The morning sun will send warm, comforting rays down through the canopy. She'll climb out of the tree, stretch her tired body, and start walking.

Perhaps she'll find a stream to follow. People often live close to water, she reasons. In her mind, she hears a babbling brook with clear, refreshing water.

The creek leads her from the forest to a clearing where a lone cabin stands. A family lives there. Astonished faces greet her as she stumbles out from the woods. They rush to her aid as she falls to her knees in sweet relief.

Sandra holds on to this vision, wishing it into existence. Her body begins violently trembling as the sweat on it cools.

A slight lean from her upright position makes her jerk awake. In her fatigue, she'd nodded off.

She moans with the terror of how awful that could have been.

Just because she no longer hears the wolves below doesn't mean they aren't there. A fall from this height won't cause much damage, but it would more than likely make her a meal.

Her heavy eyelids slump lower once more. Exhaustion and cold leave her body numb.

She needs sleep if she's to continue pressing forward in the morning. But how to get it? The threat of toppling to the hard forest floor leaves her wary to close her eyes again. If only she had a rope, something to help hold her on.

A thought comes to mind with a satisfying "aha!". The tree trunk isn't huge. Her arms almost fit all the way around it.

Moving slowly so as not to lose her balance, she unhooks her bra. Holding one end for dear life, she flings the other around the trunk and catches it on the opposite side. She puts her arms through the straps as far as they will go and prays the tension is enough to at least wake her before she drops to her death.

Eventually, she drifts off into a troubled sleep.

* * *

A wolf howls, and a gunshot answers.

A gunshot?

Her eyes fling open. In the deep dark of the night, she has no way of knowing what time it is.

A gunshot means a person, and they probably aren't more than a couple hundred yards away from the sound of it.

Indecision wars within her. If it's him, she wants to be as quiet as possible and pray he doesn't find her. If it isn't him, and who else would be out at this hour in these wolf-ridden woods, she should cry out for help.

Realism wins over optimism. The odds are slim to none that it's anyone but him.

With a dread that permeates to her core, she squeezes her eyes shut, settles her forehead back against the tree, and focuses on being silent and still.

Minutes later, footfalls tromp towards her tree, cracking the dry, fallen twigs on the forest floor. A chill runs through her, paralyzing her in place when he speaks just a few feet beneath and behind her.

The tattling beam of a flashlight falls on her naked skin.

"Good job, Bear." His voice is cheerful. "You found our little birdie."

The light blinds her when she tries to look at him, and she swivels her face back to the chafing bark.

A heavy thing clanks as it's set down. He whistles as he moves about.

A loud blow and crack sends a scream to her throat. She stifles all but a throat noise and hugs the diminishing safety of the trunk tighter.

An object slithers across the ground. Snaps and other noises precede a persistent crackling and popping.

Unable to bear the not knowing, she turns her head and strains to see behind her without loosening her hold on the tree. A whiff of smoke burns her nose and eyes.

A small fire dances below, casting red flickers on his gleeful face. He leans back against a large backpack, a cigarette hanging from his lips. A rifle lays across his lap, and his giant German Shepherd rests with his muzzle on the man's knee.

Their eyes meet.

"Well, hello there, Sandra." He smiles up at her in a casual way, like someone happening upon an old friend while walking down the street.

She turns back to the tree, her body trembling. Her breath comes in great hitching gasps. Icy tendrils of despair invade every fiber of her being.

A horrid realization sprouts and blooms in her mind. When she'd run out of the cabin, he stayed behind. Got dressed. Spent the extra minutes to pack. He'd been willing to chance the wolves hunting her down first.

And now, she's freezing in a tree, in her underpants, while he's cozy by the fire below. A rush of hot fury burns through her, only to fizzle out in no time as the weight of terror resettles.

The warm glow of light in her peripheral vision brings a slight comfort from the oppressive darkness of the night. At the same time, the hope of finding anyone to help her fades.

In the morning, she will be no safer to climb down than when she climbed up.

"What's the matter, Sandra?" he goads. "You don't feel like talking? You were definitely talkative when you were lying in my bed."

His words bring the memory of his hands on her back to the forefront of her mind, and she shudders. What she wouldn't give to be able to wash his body oils from her.

Prickles crawl across her skin, but she doesn't dare release the tree to scratch them away. Instead, she presses against the trunk, not caring how it scrapes at her face.

Desperation lodges in her throat. She makes a promise to herself. No matter what happens, he won't touch her ever again.

"Goodnight, Sandra."

Asshole.

9

The Abduction

"Sandra, table ten said 'no' to dessert. They're ready for the check. They've got a movie to catch." Becky passes Sandra with the table's empty plates.

"Good." Sandra leaves the cleaning towel on table twelve as she goes to print the bill for ten. "I've got a movie to catch, too."

The first thing Sandra said to her co-workers when she walked into work that evening was that she wanted to be the first to leave. She'd closed the front of the restaurant enough times recently to deserve it, and she had a late-night movie date at the theater with her best friend, Kim.

"What are you going to see?" Becky deposits the dishes with a clank into the nearby bus tub.

Sandra pauses to answer. "Seven Days in Barcelona. It's supposed to be this really steamy, passionate movie about a girl who goes on vacation to Barcelona by herself to prove to her family she can be independent and ends up being swept off her feet by a sexy Spaniard."

"You're such a romantic." Becky laughs and pushes a dish towel into Sandra's hands. "When are you going to get yourself a boyfriend?"

Sandra purses her lips thoughtfully. "When I meet a nice guy." She turns and takes the little black guest check folder and two mints to table ten. To her relief, they have their credit card ready.

She finishes cleaning her section and rolling her share of the silverware while waiting for her last table to leave. It only takes a few minutes for her to settle her books for the night and tip out the hostess.

After clocking out, she grabs her coat and purse. With a quick wave to her co-workers, she heads out into the crisp March evening.

The little bistro she works at is located in a residential district. The alleyway she walks down to get to the street she parks on isn't well-lit, but she isn't that worried. She's worked here for two years now and hasn't heard of much crime in the area. As she comes out of the dark alley, she's greeted by the glow of the streetlamp she parked near.

Usually, she isn't bothered by going out to her car alone. But tonight, the shadows seem to be especially long and jagged. A white cargo van, parked across the street from her car, is the only other vehicle on the block.

After a glance left and right down the empty street, she crosses and presses the unlock button on the keys. As she opens the driver's door, something heavy slams into her upper back.

The surprise blow knocks the breath from her and drops her to the ground. Sandra rolls on the hard concrete in pain and confusion, coughing and gasping as her lungs struggle to expand. She squints up against the light at a man in a blue ski mask bending down over her.

"Help," she whimpers, unable to muster any force behind the

word.

He grabs one wrist roughly, shoves her onto her stomach, and secures her hands behind her back with the yank of a zip tie. The stranger crams a handkerchief in her mouth with two of his broad fingers and a sharp grip on her jaw before locking it in with a piece of tape. A stifling hood comes down over her face, obscuring her vision. Cords in the bottom of the fabric are pulled until they are uncomfortably snug around her neck.

Despite the tightness encircling her throat, she's able to catch a full breath. Fueled by the oxygen, Sandra wriggles and bucks against the restraints, but they hold fast. Her heart pounds like a warning bell in her temples.

Is this happening?

Her tongue pushes against the gag without succeeding in anything. Muffled screams sound in her throat but don't carry. Frantically, she squirms, but he holds her fast.

With barely any effort or even much of a grunt, he swings her over his shoulder like a side of beef.

Sandra tries to kick him, but he pins her legs in his arms. Pressing her head toward his back with the thought to bite, she can't even get her teeth on his shirt with the thick cloth in her mouth.

After maybe twenty steps, a gritty noise squeals like a squeaky door opening. She spends a moment in the air before landing on the metal floor of a cargo bay. Her shoulder connects with the hard surface first and blooms with a fresh agony.

The van creaks as he climbs inside. Barely any air remains in her empty lungs, but she uses it as fuel to kick at him. Like subduing a small puppy, he grips each foot in turn, slams them against the floor, and tightly secures her ankles together.

The plastic digs into her wrists as she strains, trying to free herself. She tries to speak through the gag and tape, to plead with him to let her go, but all that comes out is muffled, garbled nonsense.

He kicks her in the stomach. The instant spasm of misery takes her air away, and she scrunches into a tense ball. His boot connects with her butt, and her body jerks in an opposite motion.

Then he leaves her, closing the back of the van behind him, and makes his way to the driver's seat.

Tears stream down her cheeks as the vehicle begins to move. She slams her feet against the metal side panel and throws her shoulder against it to no avail. Tense knots tighten in her chest and stomach mirroring the physical restraints.

* * *

As the pain in her belly and ass start to subside, Sandra searches for options. How can she get her hands free? The plastic around them is excruciatingly tight to begin with.

Her entire life has been spent reading and watching romances. Survival situations don't often come up in that genre.

Somewhere in her memory, she recalls someone getting out of handcuffs by dislocating their thumb. Even if that would work in this situation, she doesn't know how to do that or if she's desperate enough to try. Yet.

Thinking back to a self-defense class she took with Kim years ago, she remembers you can saw through a zip tie with a shoelace. But your hands need to be in front of you.

She rolls around, her shoes banging loudly on the metal floor, searching for anything she can use to free her hands or to assist herself with.

The van picks up speed as if it's on the highway. She whimpers in distress, wondering how far he intends to take her. Violent tremors shake her, increasing with each passing second that they travel further away from where she's supposed to be.

Every movement in her journey exploring the back of the vehicle makes her shoulders ache from the unnatural position. The zip ties dig into her flesh, causing her wrists to chafe and bleed. The moisture isn't enough to help her slip them off though. Her struggle is fruitless; the cargo area is completely clean and all the surfaces she can reach are smooth.

Despair presses down on her like a trash compactor crushing her into a tiny cube. Fresh sobs shake her.

But she can't live with this dread. She must regroup to brainstorm her next plan of action.

The van's speed reduces.

Sandra gasps for oxygen as panic threatens to smother her.

They navigate a couple of turns and come to a stop. The driver's door opens and closes with a deafening clang. The van sways with the shifting weight.

Sandra concentrates on breathing calmly and evenly to hear what's going on outside. *What is he doing? Are other people near? Is he going to hurt me?*

The back of the van squeals as it opens. With nowhere to go, she recoils and worms for a corner.

He grabs one of her ankles and yanks her from the vehicle, allowing her body to topple to the ground. Her head smacks into solid dirt. She cries out, the sound muffled by the gag. A metallic taste fills her mouth from biting her tongue.

She moans and rolls off her tender shoulder onto her stomach. Fresh sobbing hitches shake her. She doesn't want to give him the pleasure of seeing her cry, but she can't help herself.

Something small and hard presses into her side. Her body jerks and tenses involuntarily. She's unable to move as electricity floods her nervous system. Piercing electrical darts attack every square inch of her body and rattle around in her skull. The hurt goes on forever until it finally ends.

Please, don't do that again; I'll do anything if you don't.

But he does.

An invisible vice grips her spine while her body twitches violently. She's helpless, unable to cry any louder than a strangled gurgle.

After an eternity, it ceases once again. Her throat is thick with sobs. Each muscle aches as if it's been released from a Charlie horse. A wet warmness spreads across her crotch from her bladder letting go.

He hoists her up and tosses her back into the van with another painful thump. Never had she imagined finding relief in that, but she does now.

The door screeches and slams with a thud. The vehicle rocks as he returns to the wheel. The engine starts, and they move again.

Her mind searches for any meaning behind what's just happened. Was it a warning? Punishment for moving around?

Don't let it break you, she tells herself. For now, she'll remain still and try to keep calm.

With nothing to hold her attention, the movement of the van eventually lulls her exhausted body into a light sleep.

* * *

Her swollen eyes break through the crust of dried tears to fly open when the vehicle comes to a stop. A rush of nervous, tense energy courses through her. She still can't see anything with the hood over her face. The cloth is stale from her breath and sweat.

Her ears strain, hoping to detect a sign that other humans are near, praying for a friendly voice that might aid her. Sandra pivots on her bruised butt until she's in a position to bang her feet against the walls and waits, bracing for an opportunity to alert someone of her presence.

When she feels him get out, her heart begins pounding. Where is he going? Is he coming back to hurt her again? Involuntarily, she cringes and whines.

The silence and waiting are unbearable. Every nerve waits on edge for information about his location.

After a few minutes, her attention shifts to her arms and shoulders which ache from her hands being bound behind her. She wiggles her fingers to make sure they're still receiving blood flow. They're stiff with cold.

Her heartbeat is the only signal of passing time; and eventually, that too slows as nothing happens.

As quietly as possible, she rolls her body over to the wall to put her ear up against it. Again, nothing.

Don't lose heart, Sandra.

As she begins to pull away, there's a distant, muffled hum of what could be a semi.

They're still near a road.

A small flicker of hope lights within her as she realizes they'll need to stop for gas at some point. People will be there. She can bang on the walls then.

The van rocks and the engine starts. A potty break, most likely.

There's no way to know what time it is. If he stops to refuel in the middle of the night or in the wee hours of the morning, chances are no one else will be around.

Sandra recalls a news report of an abduction of a little girl. The girl's parents were filmed with a message for the kidnapper. They used their daughter's name a lot and kept repeating what a kind, caring person she was, as they begged for her safe return.

If only Sandra could get her own abductor to take the gag off her and permit her to speak. Perhaps she could humanize herself, convince him not to hurt her anymore. Maybe he would let her go.

Every minute is another mile further from home. What did Kim do when Sandra never showed up for the movie? How long before someone calls the police?

Her co-workers must have noticed her parked car when they left work. They might have assumed Kim picked her up, and that Sandra would get her vehicle after the movie.

Are there any traffic cameras that could have seen the abduction? She never thought to look. Is anyone searching for this van?

Madness and despair fight to squash the little glimmer of hope she seeks to protect like a candle flame in a storm.

She shivers and curls into a ball. Between her damp pants and the metal floor, she trembles with unbearable cold. The treatment reduces her to feeling like an animal in a trap, ready to chew through her leg for freedom. Only, she isn't permitted the opportunity to do even that desperate action.

Now that the visual is trapped in her mind, she wonders if she could bring herself to mutilate herself like that.

Sleep would be a relief, but she's wide awake and uncomfortable. The long night hours drag on and on.

The van stops again. From the slight screech of a metal hinge, she guesses they're at a refueling pitstop. Unable to detect other people nearby, she stays quiet. A few short minutes later, they're back on the road. Her glimmer of hope dims further.

Tears leak from and burn the edges of her eyes as she realizes how far from home she must be. Sandra offers a silent prayer that she'll see her home and family again.

Eventually, she dozes off.

* * *

The back door of the van squealing wakes her up. Disoriented and groggy, Sandra blinks against the filtered light leaking through the hood. Her bruised body aches in places she never knew could ache.

The glow through the fabric over her head makes her wonder if it's morning. She listens for sounds of possible help nearby, but he seems too smart to risk that.

The van rocks as he climbs into the back, grabs her arm, and drags her to the opening. The movement is painful on her sore shoulders and chafed wrists; she lets out a muffled cry.

He loosens the cord around her neck, reaches in without taking the hood off, and rips the tape from her face. The tender flesh of her lips and face burns where the tape had been for so many long hours. Fresh air filters in from the neck hole of the hood. With a little assistance from him, she spits the gag out and takes a few gasping breaths.

"Thank you." The words tumble out. Relief from being able to speak and breathe freely relaxes her slightly. The welcome unwinding is short-lived as a burning shame accompanies the expression of gratitude to her attacker. It's his fault she's here and in pain and terror instead of at home, safe in her bed. Thoughts of home and bed bring new tears to her eyes.

Why does he deserve thanks?

The cord of the hood over her head is tightened again. The fresh air dissipates. What is it he doesn't want her to see? Or is the lack of vision meant to keep her more fearful? Could she possibly be more afraid than she already is?

Gathering the courage to speak, to humanize herself, she swallows and begins, "My name is–"

As she opens her mouth, he slips something else over her head and tightens it around her neck. Her words are cut off by a noose that jerks her from the van and up into the air.

Instantly, breathing becomes impossible. Blood pounds in her brain. She bucks and instinctively tries to swing her body about, choking and gurgling. The darkness inside the hood deepens.

All leftover strength drains from her, and she stills.

The tension above her releases, and she falls, landing hard on her bound ankles. Her right ankle gives way with a loud pop, and pain shoots up her leg. Sandra tumbles to the ground screaming.

Her shriek gradually turns into a sob which fades into a whimper of despair. The first lucid thought she has is that he took the gag out because he wanted to hear her scream. The second is that there's no chance of someone hearing her pleas. It's just the two of them. She's beyond aid.

"Please," she begs, knowing she must hurry to appeal to his humanity in order to save her life.

The response to her plea is another agonizing trip back up into the air. All thoughts cease as she fights against her restraints to stay alive.

Again, he waits until she stills before releasing her to the ground. She doesn't try to stick the landing and collapses.

When her breathing stabilizes, she determines to get her name out. Even if it means he'll hang her again. She needs to know she tried everything.

"Cassandra," she moans. Not knowing if he heard or not, she braces herself for one more attempt. "Cassandra," she says a little louder.

Once more, she's dragged by her neck into the air. The world goes dark before she comes back down again.

* * *

When Sandra awakes, she notices her hands are no longer secured behind her back. Her shoulders are flat and supported. The hood is still over her head. She can't decide if his goal is to heighten her fear by blinding her, or to avoid being forced to see her human face. Could he look her in the eyes and still do such horrible things to her?

She's lying on a hard wooden surface. Her wrists and ankles are restrained to the board by cold metal cuffs.

It takes her a moment to realize the whimpering noise she hears is coming from her. Once aware of it, she attempts to calm herself by breathing in for the count of four, holding for four, exhaling for four, and repeating until she steadies. Box breathing is something she learned from yoga class. She repeats the process for a few more rounds.

This helps distract her from the overwhelming anguish. There's no part of her, internal or external, that doesn't hurt. Her throat is raw and burning. Her wrists and ankles are chafed. Every little wiggle or adjustment sends pain shooting up her leg from her right ankle. No matter how still she tries to be, her entire body aches and throbs.

Sandra tests each restraint in turn, seeing if any have the slightest give, but it's to no avail. One moment, a suffocating terror tightens her chest, threatening to take away her ability to breathe. The next, a numb apathy encourages her to give in and let go. Further struggles are no use. The two feelings alternate and overlap in a cruel tug of war.

After getting her breathing under control, she concentrates on listening for any clues as to where she is.

Everything is quiet.

She tests her restraints again, especially the ones on her wrists. If the metal holding them is screwed or nailed down, then there's a chance it can be wiggled loose.

The metal isn't as biting as the zip ties were, but it's more disconcerting. Anyone can go to a local hardware store and buy heavy-duty zip ties. What kind of person has a board to restrain people just lying around?

She rocks her body back and forth to get a feel of how big and sturdy the board might be.

It doesn't move an inch.

Her blood runs cold. This isn't his first time, unless he's been plotting and planning her abduction for a while. The preparation is too calculated for an amateur.

She's more exposed and vulnerable than when she was alone in the back of the van.

Now, she;s nearly spread eagle, restrained to some kind of bed or table with a psychopath undoubtedly nearby. Her struggles become frantic. The only way out of this is to save herself. Help isn't coming. He drove for so long that they're clearly out in the middle of nowhere. The lack of a gag sends the message loud and clear that no one is around to hear her.

She pulls and strains and twists but nothing gives. A wail of terror and pain escapes through her clenched teeth despite her best efforts to contain it. She doesn't want him to know that she's awake but can't stop.

After a few more rounds of box breaths to slow the runaway pace of her heart, Sandra focuses on the metal holding her right wrist and begins working it. Her attention zeros in until it's the only thing she's thinking about.

Back and forth. The movement is slight but satisfying. Having something to focus on brings a little stillness to her mind.

The scabbed wounds from the zip tie break open and bleed. The pain is excruciating, but she can't think about that. It's up to her to save herself. Help isn't coming. The agony is worth it.

When a hand falls on her thigh, she freezes.

He's been right there, watching her all along.

* * *

"Please," escapes her lips instinctually, but she doesn't want to beg. He might enjoy that. It's important to tell him about herself. Talking hurts, but she has no other strategy at the moment.

Composing herself, she starts anew. "My name is Cassandra Grayson. I'm only 24 years old." Her mind races, searching for the right words. Scouring for information that will humanize her. "I like animals. I have a cat named Minny who's going to miss me when I don't come home."

She groans inwardly at the stupid thoughts her desperation drums up. *Talk about your family, not your cat.* "My mom and dad will miss me. I had a date planned tonight with my best friend Kim. We've been friends since the second grade."

This is good. He must be listening, 'cause he isn't saying anything. I could be getting through.

A scraping noise, like two metal objects sliding against each other, answers her. The first sound she's heard since she awoke that could have been made by him.

Her heart beats like a prisoner trying to escape the bars of her ribcage. Could that have been a key sliding as he picked it up? Is he going to let her go?

"I like romance books and movies. And taking long walks on the beach." *This isn't a personal ad, Sandra.* "My favorite food is pizza." She kicks herself internally, realizing she's rambling in her panic, but it's the first chance she's gotten to actually talk to him without pain immediately following.

A small sliver of cold metal touches her ankle under the hem of her jeans. At the contact, she twitches and recoils. What new torture does he have planned?

"Please." The word tumbles out again, making her cheeks burn. A tear escapes the corner of her eye. "I want to go home."

In the otherwise stillness, metal swooshes along metal. A snip precedes the falling away of denim from her leg. The cool object moves up a couple of inches. A chilling realization assaults her—he is cutting her pants off.

"No. Don't do this." She yanks against her restraints to no avail. *Is he going to rape me?*

All of her previous experiences with sex have been awkward and clumsy, even to the point of embarrassing and uncomfortable. At seventeen, her persistent boyfriend had convinced her to give him her virginity in the backseat of his car in a closed Dairy Queen drive-thru at midnight. The encounter was unfulfilling and left her with a sticky, smelly mess to clean up using only the couple of napkins found in a paper takeout bag beneath the seat. After two similar incidents over the next two weeks, they broke up.

In the seven years since, her friends, especially Kim, had been trying to set her up with "nice guys". Sandra would go out with anyone at least once. She dated one for a month, and they had sex a few times, but no one ignited a fire in her the way the male protagonists did in the books she read.

She was looking for "the one" who would sweep her off her feet.

After one drink too many, she had slept with a guy on their first date and was hurt and shocked when it turned into a one-night stand. After that, she swore to wait.

The blade of the scissors tickles her thigh as he lengthens the slit in her jeans. Methodical in his actions, he takes his time.

Her stomach turns. He's enjoying this. The bastard is actually enjoying every moment.

A whimper escapes her. "Please. Stop."

The scissors snake their way across her panties and cut through the waistband of her jeans. Then she feels them against her other ankle, making their way up her right leg.

With one more half-hearted tug at the metal bands holding her down, Sandra resigns to her fate. She doesn't want to increase his pleasure with her pleadings.

With a sigh, she turns her head away from him.

When her jeans have become two pieces, he pulls them from her body. Her damp, clammy flesh breaks out in goosebumps. Her heart races as she pictures herself lying on a table, mostly naked from the waist down. She knows the effect this must have on him.

Her face burns.

His fingers trace the curves of her legs from her ankles, across her calves, up her thighs; she tries to recoil but is unable to go anywhere.

His hand lifts.

Sandra waits in the darkness of the hood over her head

knowing he is standing over her, watching her, thinking of his next step while biding his time and taking it slow. She can't see anything through the fabric, not even the shape of him. However, she can almost feel his lingering shadow.

The delay sends her thoughts into a frenzy. The lack of urgency is worrying. Disturbing. Agony.

He must have honed and practiced this scene countless times before. How many girls has he kidnapped to be this well-rehearsed, to have this much self-control?

Like a traitor revealing secrets, her body trembles.

The waiting is a new kind of torment, wondering what he'll do next. Her ears search for any sounds over her own labored breathing, echoing inside the hood. Every time she thinks she's regained enough composure to pause and listen, her breath quickens. Her heart pounds against her breastbone and pulses in her head.

Dread and a twisted relief flood together when the scissors touch her wrist. The edge of her sleeve lifts. While the knowing is temporarily better than the unknowing, fresh panic sets in.

The fabric of her shirt gives way between the two blades. She dares not move with sharp metal near the thinnest parts of her skin. He cuts from the sleeves in and then from the hem up. Her shirt is jerked from her torso, leaving her in her bra and panties.

She shivers.

And waits.

The waiting gnaws at her, making her insides ache. Why does he pause? There had been no sound of him going away, meaning he's standing over her defenseless body, drilling holes into her with his eyes.

Her skin crawls like someone dumped a bucket of ants on her.

With a determined struggle, she holds her breath for a moment. At first, she hears nothing. Then her ears catch the faintest sound of an exhale.

Something within her snaps at the soft, controlled noise. Sandra lets out a gut-wrenching scream and twists and bucks against the restraints.

She screams until her throat is hoarse. Maybe no one's around to hear, but she must release some of the pent-up terror twisting knots in her chest or go mad from it.

Why doesn't he laugh, gloat, or make any sound, even a whisper? Give her some indication, any at all, that he is human rather than a monstrous demon. Could the torments of a mystical hell be worse than the silence of her captor?

"Why won't you say something?" she pants into the darkness when she's regained some semblance of control. "Can you speak?"

He must know how his lack of words contributes to the distress of his victims, another sign that the perpetrator has a history of these horrific crimes.

There's no way out of this. The thought creeps into her mind like a silent shadow in a horror film. She searches for a shred of hope. It's slipping from her like the heat leaving her uncovered skin.

His hand grasps her wrist, and she gasps and jerks.

Something pointed presses into the soft flesh of her arm beneath the elbow and breaks the skin. Slowly, he rakes the knife down her arm, cutting a shallow gash into her. Blood dribbles from the hot wound.

Sandra screams at this sharp, biting pain. She imagines him relishing her torment, but she's helpless to stop her reaction.

The small blade lifts; she tries to catch her breath. A thin stream of blood trickles down her arm. She fights another round of panic.

"Why?" Pleading is useless, but she can't stop herself from asking. This must be a monster, not a human, she is certain now. What kind of human could do this to another and enjoy it?

The tip of the knife touches her stomach. Every muscle in her tenses, bracing for the inevitable. She knows it would hurt less if she could relax more, but that is beyond her control.

Methodically, the knife twists and carves and swoops as if he is practicing calligraphy on her belly.

She moans from nausea and focuses on breathing, counting, anything to take her mind off the searing pain. He isn't trying to bleed her out; this is some form of sick, twisted pleasure. Right now, she's nothing more than a canvas, and his scalpel is his paintbrush.

Each minute drags out like an hour. Every time the blade lifts, she wonders where it will land. Nothing is safe. He slices open the skin on her legs, her upper breasts, her face.

If she ever gets out of this, who will want her body ever again? Surely not the passionate Latin lover she desires from her romance novels. His sculpted physique requires a perfectly airbrushed body. He would take one look at these future scars and turn away in disgust.

Sandra weeps for her losses. The loss of the perfect lover who will show her the pleasures of sex as she's never experienced them before. The loss of a doting husband and adorable baby they will make together if she doesn't survive on the cold, metal table.

She weeps for the loss her parents and Kim will feel if she disappears without a trace. This madman is going to dump her in the middle of nowhere to rot and never be found.

The pain that never ends brings her to the verge of puking.

Bile burns the back of her throat. Her head swims.

As a defense mechanism, her body begins to shut down. One minute, she drifts on a dark sea of unconsciousness. The next, searing agony accompanies the splitting of her flesh.

The carving stops.

She holds her breath, waiting. Tensing though it tears at the cuts in her skin.

The pause lights her nerves in horrifying anticipation.

The knife sinks deep into her thigh. Tendrils of torment shoot up and down her leg.

Sandra can't quit screaming until she passes out.

* * *

At first, Sandra is too delirious to tell if the sensation of being dragged by her feet is a dream or reality. The hood, secured about her neck, still covers her head.

Her body slides over grass; every now and then a twig or branch provides resistance and scratches her bare skin.

I'm free of the table, she thinks as she wriggles her wrists.

Her feet are not free, however. She's being dragged by a rope that binds them.

Filtered light strobes her face as they pass patches of sunlight through the trees.

Where is he taking me? She's too tired to fight or resist. He must know this because her hands are unbound. She tries to lift one but doesn't have the strength.

Is this what dying feels like? The thought is strangely comforting now. At least it would be a way to escape. He'd been planning her slow death all along, and now that it's here, she's surprisingly unafraid.

The dragging continues, and her back becomes chafed and raw. The discomfort is more of a nuisance as the other injuries capture most of her attention. Her ankles hurt the worst with the constant pressure of the rope digging into them, deepening their wounds.

Sandra drifts in and out of awareness. Finally, they stop. He drops her legs to the ground.

And walks away.

His footsteps fade off into the distance. Soon, the only sound she hears is a few birds whistling in the trees.

Can she really be free from him? Is this some new, cruel trick? The hope of relief floods her eyes with tears.

With a great effort, she brings her arms down and tries to untie the cord around her neck that holds the hood in place. Her fingers fumble at the knot, but they don't have the strength to release it. It feels like an eternity since she's seen anything beyond the dark fabric. The possibility that she will die with it on is overwhelming. Her breath and heartbeat quicken with the terror of it, but only slightly and not for long. Little by little, her body is shutting down.

Sandra licks her lips but it does nothing to soothe them. Little moisture remains in her. She has no way of knowing how long she'd been in his possession, but she's clearly dehydrated.

An insane giggle escapes. Maybe that will kill her before he can finish her off.

She twists her head about, wondering which direction she should crawl. His footsteps had faded away to her left. That probably isn't the way she wants to go. Unless he was walking back toward a road. There's no way she'll be able to traverse the distance she was dragged in her condition. Help needs to be closer than that to do her any good.

To the right it is.

With a great effort, Sandra rolls from her back to her front. Even if she had the strength to walk, her right ankle wouldn't support her weight. The pressure of the ground against it is excruciating. Each tremor ignites a new wave of misery up her leg.

Since she can't get the hood off her head, it's safer to crawl. No chance of tripping over a rock or a tree root if she's already on the ground.

It's time to get moving. Her senses are on high alert, astute to any sign that he might be coming back. It would be like him to make her think this reprieve is permanent. Even if she dies out in these woods, she wants to get far enough away that he can't find her.

One weak arm stretches out and grasps a tuft of grass. She pushes her elbow against the cool soil and lurches forward an inch or two.

Every twig and rock beneath her tugs and rips at the wounds in her split skin. But she can't stop.

Her other hand reaches out and repeats the process.

Within minutes, she pauses to catch her breath and allows her racing pulse to slow. Dehydration and blood loss are making her heart work twice as hard. She doesn't have enough water in her to sweat. The overwhelming effort might have resulted in a couple of feet of progress.

Exhaustion and despair fade to black.

10

Found

Somewhere far away, someone whistles. Sandra latches on to the noise like it's a lifeline and pulls herself to consciousness. A person is nearby.

Him. The word comes unbidden to her mind. But maybe it isn't him. The only sounds she ever heard from *him* while he held her captive were his breathing and his footsteps.

"Haaa...." She attempts to call out help, but all that exits her desiccated throat is a weak, dry gasp.

The whistling stops.

She holds her breath. Has he gone away? Did she only imagine hearing someone?

"Bear? Where are you going?" a male voice calls out.

The human voice is the most wonderful thing she's heard since she was kidnapped.

"Gaaa..." she tries again to alert whoever it is. This second try was a little louder but had no possibility of carrying through the woods.

"Come back, Bear," the man says, sounding a little closer than before.

The repetition of the word "bear" causes her alarm. He couldn't be talking about a real bear, could he?

Moments later, soft feet pad towards her, accompanied by a rapid sniffing. A wet nose touches her hand, and a large slobbery tongue licks her arm. The dog whines as if in empathy.

The man's footsteps crunch from nearby.

"Oh my God, Bear, what did you find?" He hastens to kneel next to her and checks her wrist for a pulse. "Woah, she's still alive." His hands fumble at her neck to undo the cords.

Relief washes over her as the hood is lifted off her head. She inhales fresh, cool air with the sweet scent of grass.

"Miss, what happened to you?"

The sunlight is blinding. She squints her eyes against it, opening them a little at a time as they adjust.

"Bear, let her be." The man softly scolds the dog.

As if he'd decided it was his duty to clean her wounds, Bear backs off from licking her arms after one more good tongue swipe.

Gentle hands check her neck and spine before carefully rolling her over. She blinks into the light and looks up into the most beautiful brown eyes she's ever seen. A ray of sun through the trees lights a halo around his dark caramel hair.

Sandra is too weak to cry, but she stretches out a hand to touch his knee to see if he's real. He is—her fingers reach his solid build.

"Miss, are you okay?"

No. She is far from okay, but at least she's better now that he found her. Maybe the nightmare can be over. Maybe he'll help her get to safety before the maniac returns to finish her off.

The man takes his large backpack from his shoulders and sets it on the ground. He lifts a canteen strap from around his neck.

"You look awful parched. I'm going to prop you up so I can help you drink, all right?"

Sandra manages to move her head up and down a little. As carefully as he can, he pulls her against his torso and cradles her there with one arm. The pain is intense, but the warmth of his body is soothing. He smells clean.

At first, he gives her just a sip of water, only enough to wet her mouth. She moans as he takes it away, her insides screaming out for more.

"You've got to take it slow. It won't feel pleasant if you sick it back up." Over the next few minutes, he holds her and permits her several more sips. All too soon, he sets the canteen aside.

"We gotta focus on getting you indoors now. The woods aren't the safest after dark." He digs around in his crammed pack and pulls out an emergency blanket. Eyeing her wounds critically, he wraps her up. "None of these are actively bleeding. I think they can wait until we get you back to the cabin." He lowers her to the ground. "Don't worry. I'm not going far. I need to tie some branches together for a little travois to put you on."

Panic claws at Sandra's throat. She struggles against the screams and tears that build with the sound of his footsteps walking away. Relief comes in the form of a large German Shepherd. Bear settles down next to her and lays his giant head on her torso. The pain of the pressure is worth the tradeoff for the comfort.

The warmth of the dog and blanket lull her into a groggy state. She's slightly aware when she's moved onto the travois before drifting into an almost peaceful sleep.

* * *

A familiar popping and crackling from a wood fire pulls her back to reality. She imagined she'd wake up in a hospital or be on her way to one. Instead, she finds herself in a snug, one-room cabin, lying on a bed with an IV in her arm.

The man who found her in the woods stands at a small stove a few feet away, stirring something in a shiny stockpot. The savory aroma of chicken and vegetables causes her stomach to rumble. He turns as if he heard it.

"You're awake." He crosses the bit of space and draws a wooden chair close. "How are you feeling?"

With great effort, she manages to mutter, "Better."

"Good," he says with a kind chuckle. "I hoped I gave you enough Percocet."

She glances around the room without moving her head. "Where?"

He places a hand over hers. "My cabin. Don't worry. You're safe. I'm not going to hurt you. The nearest hospital is a couple hundred miles away, and I don't have a vehicle or a phone."

She raises her eyebrows in question, tension rising within her.

"It's a long story", he deflects. "We can talk about it when you're a little stronger. Would you like to try to eat something?"

"Yes," she rasps.

He hops to his feet and revisits the stove. "I made chicken soup, though I think you should start with broth." After a quick stir, he returns to her. "I'm going to very carefully move you to a sitting position. You just relax and let me do the work."

With the skill of a nurse, he props her up without causing too much pain. He gently repositions the pillows he had under her foot to elevate it.

Sandra looks down at herself, frowning. A baggie t-shirt and sweatpants replace her soiled undergarments. She's been washed, and the worst of her wounds are covered. Her swollen ankle has been wrapped.

"How?" She holds up her hand with the IV needle in it, inspecting it with wonder

"I used to be a medic in the military. I keep pretty extensive first aid supplies on hand because of how remote it is out here."

Sandra nods, absorbing the information at the speed of flowing molasses. Her brain still feels addled.

"Let's get you that soup." He dishes up a bowl and sits down next to her on the bed, her body tipping toward him as the mattress shifts.

She gazes at the steaming, golden-brown liquid, and her stomach rumbles. After what she assumes has been days since she's eaten, she's ravenous.

"It's hot." He scoops up a spoonful, blows on it twice, and brings it to her mouth.

The salty, savoriness is warm and comforting. It's as good for her emotionally as it is physically, the liquid gold warming her soul. Swallowing is difficult with her throat so swollen and raw, but it's worth the discomfort.

The process of feeding her is slow, but he doesn't rush nor does he ever seem impatient. Tears slip from her eyes and slide down her cheek. The relief of being free of her tormentor and having someone take care of her is overwhelming.

"Hey, now. There's no need for that." He drops the spoon into the bowl and brings up a napkin to dab her cheeks.

"Sorry," she breathes in embarrassment.

"There's no need for apologies either."

Overcome with fatigue, she closes her eyes. A noose chokes her throat and yanks her into the air by her neck. A knife draws lines in her skin. She stops breathing. Her body trembles as she relives it.

"Open your eyes. Whatever you're seeing isn't real anymore." He sets the dish on the side table and takes her hand.

Blinking back the memory, Sandra manages to free herself from the flashback and meets his gaze. Care and concern shine in the kind brown eyes looking back at her.

His brows lift in a sudden realization. "How about some Valium? That might help you relax."

She nods her head and whispers, "Okay." This stranger has been kind to her so far. Perhaps he can be trusted. Either way, she doesn't have much of a choice.

From some drawers across the room, he retrieves a vial, measures a dose into a syringe, and administers it into her IV line. "That should feel better real soon."

The drug takes the edge off enough for her to close her eyes without reliving the recent brutality. Darkness and quiet overtake her.

* * *

When she wakes up, the room is dark, except for the warm glow coming from the fireplace. Soft snoring echoes off the walls from the direction of the light.

She wishes she could go back to sleep, but a pressing need to empty her bladder nags. When her eyes adjust to the dimness, she notices two doors. One is across the cabin, and judging by what she thinks is a coat rack near it, it must be a door to outside. The other is closer, and she hopes it leads to a bathroom. How to get to it is the question.

At this point, she's willing to crawl if she has to. Her cheeks burn in humiliation at the memory of lying in a puddle of her urine. That can't happen again.

When she tries to move her elevated ankle, excruciating agony shoots up her leg and takes her breath away. It definitely won't support any of her weight.

The snoring pauses for a moment in response to her noise and then resumes. She hates to wake whoever's sleeping, especially because she isn't sure who it is. A dim recollection of a person feeding her spoonfuls of homemade soup comes to mind. The remembrance of someone finding her in the woods brings her some hope that she's safe, but she doesn't understand why she would be at someone's dwelling and not in a hospital.

The need to pee grows more urgent.

Besides her ankle, she would also have to navigate the cabin with an active IV. Following its tubing up above her head, she sees it isn't on a handy metal stand with wheels that she might have used as a crutch, but rather hangs on a hook on the wall. Getting it off would be its own feat. How would she carry it with her to the bathroom?

The more she thinks about it, the more she realizes she's not going to be able to do this by herself. With a knot of embarrassment in her gut, she calls out, "Hello?"

Well, she thought she was calling out. What came out of her raw, swollen throat sounded more like the croak of a dying frog. After a painful attempt at a throat clearing, she tries again and manages to be a little louder.

The snores stop again, and this time, the couch springs creak.

"Did you need something?" He speaks at a level barely above a whisper.

"Yes." Tension melts from her and tears spring to her eyes with the relief of knowing someone is there to help.

He throws back a blanket and stands up. In the glow of the

firelight, she can see he's only wearing baggy pants.

He walks to the wall near the door and uses a dimmer switch to bring some faint overhead light into the room. With soft footfalls, he moves to the bedside. "What can I get for you?"

"Need. To. Pee." Each word is difficult not only physically but emotionally. Sandra's cheeks burn.

"All right." He pauses to think for a moment, glancing between her and the door she assumed leads to the bathroom. "I'm sorry, I don't have a bedpan. I should consider putting that on the shopping list for next month. I guess I'm going to carry you. It's a good thing you look light as a feather."

He looks from her to the IV bag and back. "Do you think you can hold on to this," he sets it in her lap, "and I'll do all the rest?"

Sandra clutches it to her in answer.

He leans down and pulls her arm that's closest to him around his neck. His other arm slips under her knees.

"Easy does it." He lifts her up against his bare chest effortlessly.

The movement causes a spasm of pain in her ankle, and she gasps.

"Sorry," he whispers, his voice full of sincerity.

She shakes her head, hoping he gets the message that it isn't his fault.

With smooth and even steps, he carries her around the bed. She manages to twist the knob, and the door swings open to reveal a compact room with a toilet, a sink with a small mirror over it, and a tiny shower.

"All right, as I set you down and help you stand, your job is to keep your weight off your right ankle. Let's put that saline bag in the sink for now."

Sandra clings to his neck with what little strength she has and focuses on keeping her bum ankle off the ground.

"Okay, hang onto me and the doorway for support so I can, ummm..." His eyes drop briefly from hers as if he, too, feels her embarrassment.

Drop my drawers. She thinks the words she hasn't the ability to say and nods her head in understanding.

He turns his head as he pulls the waistband of the sweats off from the top of her hips. When the pants are around her ankles, he helps her lower to the toilet.

"If you promise you won't fall off, I'll step out and close the door for a minute. Give you some privacy."

Sandra nods.

"Rap on the side of the cabinet when you're ready."

Once the door is between them, she lets her bladder relax and empty. She's grateful to have enough arm mobility to wipe herself. When she knocks her knuckles on the wood paneling, he comes back in.

Returning her to bed is a smooth reversal of the process. As he tucks her in, gratitude swells for this kind stranger. Not only has he taken such good care of her, but he also helped her preserve as much of her dignity as possible through an entirely embarrassing situation. A few tears escape and leave a burning, salty trail down her cheeks.

"Don't cry." He wipes them away with a tissue. "I'm here for whatever you need. Would you like a little more Percocet before I go back to sleep?"

With the pressure in her bladder gone, the aches in her body scream with renewed vigor. A pain pill would probably help her sleep if she accepts. Sandra nods.

After administering the meds, he turns off the overhead light and adds another log to the fire.

Sandra settles back to sleep.

* * *

Sandra wakes up feeling surprisingly better than she expected to. After thinking about it, she realizes none of her injuries were life-threatening in and of themselves. The most severe are her swollen throat, the stab wound in her thigh, and her busted ankle. Her throat feels less constricted, and she hopes that means talking will be easier. Maybe she'll be able to get some answers from the kind stranger who's been taking such good care of her. How will she ever begin to repay him?

The mental traumas are the worst. She can see her current reality in one eye and a blue ski mask in the other. Closing either plunges her right back into the nightmare.

She lifts her left hand and looks at the cloth wrapping it. What do the wounds underneath it look like? Will they heal to leave big, ugly scars?

At least my face isn't scarred. I can move up north and forever wear long sleeves and be a crazy reclusive cat lady. She sighs.

"Oh good, you're awake."

The voice coming from the couch startles her, sending her heart on another rampant sprint.

"Sorry." He offers a regretful grimace as he gets up and comes over, setting a book he was reading on the chair nearby. "How are you feeling?"

The features on his face soften with concern. She responds with a weak smile.

"Bet-ter." Every syllable is a struggle.

Being an avid reader herself, she glances down to see what

he's reading. Her whole face lights up when she discovers it's *The Notebook* by Nicholas Sparks. She points to the book. "That's. My. Fave." Each word requires a painful effort, but she enjoys being able to get a clear point across.

"Really? I just started reading it for the first time. I'm only a few pages in. If you want me to, I can start over and read you a little after breakfast."

She nods with enthusiasm.

"Excellent. And speaking of eggs – sorry, all my jokes are corny like that – do you want some? I was hoping maybe a soft scramble would go down easy on your throat."

"Sounds. Good." A lump chokes her at how endearing it is for him to put so much thought into taking care of her.

He jumps up, lights the stove, and pulls out a pan.

"I didn't want to do anything over here before you woke up. I figured you needed your rest." He grabs a carton of eggs from a nearby pantry cupboard and notices her raised eyebrows as he swivels back. "Unwashed from the farm doesn't require refrigeration." He cracks several into a bowl.

"Hey," he says as if something has just occurred to him. "If you like the book *The Notebook*, you must like the movie, right?"

When he turns to look at her, she nods, 'yes'.

"Do you think it's super important to finish the book before watching the movie?"

She moves her eyes up and scrunches her nose in thought.

"If you have to think about it that hard then we should wait. The book doesn't seem that long and maybe we'll be able to watch the movie together after we finish it."

Sandra raises her eyebrows and glances around the cabin.

"I know what you're thinking, and I'll try to answer all your questions while you eat. These'll only take a minute."

When the eggs are done, he dishes them out of the pan, helps her sit up, and offers her the bowl.

"Do you want to try? Or I don't mind feeding you again."

"I. Think. I. Can." She holds out an unsteady arm.

He hands her the dish and sits down in the nearby chair with his own. "I'm Luke."

"Cassandra."

"Like the Trojan priestess of Apollo, right?"

Sandra blushes and smiles, appreciating the obscure refer-ence. "Right." She puts a small bite of egg in her mouth and chews it thoroughly before attempting to swallow. The process isn't as painful as she thought it would be. Her stomach growls with need.

"Being out here alone all the time, just Bear and I, I end up reading a lot. He's not a great conversationalist."

"Why? A. Lone?"

He sighs and looks down before lifting his eyes to meet hers again. She tips her chin in encouragement for him to continue.

"If I told you, I'd have to kill you." He laughs.

When her expression changes to alarm he quickly sobers.

"Oh my God. I'm such an asshole. That was a really distasteful joke." He reaches out and touches her covered knee. "I'm so used to saying whatever I want to Bear. Will you please forgive me?"

She nods and breathes to slow her quickened pulse.

"I'm out here 'cause I'm in the witness protection program. No one knows I even exist anymore. When I got out of the military, I decided I wanted something more than just a… boring civilian job, you know? After going through some extensive training, I went undercover to help take down a huge drug cartel. When my cover was blown, the government hid me out here."

He waves a hand at the simple cabin space. "The only connection I have to the outside world is my handler who drops by once a month to bring me supplies and pick up my list of items for the next round. He's not even allowed to know who I am. I go out for an all-day hike when he's scheduled to come. That's what I was doing when I found you."

Luke stops talking, and Sandra stares at him as his words sink in. His story makes sense. Though he's lived a full life for how old he looks. She wouldn't guess him to be much more than thirty-five. And if it's true, she's stuck here with him for another four weeks. Or slightly less now. She has no concept of how long she's been here.

"Did I answer all your questions?" he asks between big bites of egg.

She nods and slowly chews, trying to process and come to terms with the situation.

After making quick work of his breakfast, he replaces the plate in his hands for the nearby book. "Are we ready to get started on this? I enjoyed reading earlier and want to know what happens next."

"Yes. Please."

* * *

He reads for about an hour and closes the book with a contented sigh. After a thoughtful pause, he meets her eyes with a look of regret.

"I need to get some chores done, but first I need to change your bandages and clean your wounds."

Knowing this was coming at some point, she nods though her insides clench with trepidation.

From a nearby closet, he collects a tidy basket full of sealed linens and sets it down on the chair. He fills a small tub with water and gathers a towel, a sponge, and a fresh set of clothes for her.

Starting with her arms, he begins peeling back the dressings, revealing the spider web of knife marks to her for the first time. Ridges of light red flesh in the process of knitting itself back together swirl and intersect across the entire back of her arm.

A cry escapes her, and her eyes fill with tears.

He grimaces in empathy. "I'm sorry. This must be really difficult for you. The good news is—nothing here looks infected. Everything is healing nicely. In another week we can begin putting vitamin E oil over all of it to mitigate the scarring. Okay?"

She nods and wipes her tears.

Once both arms are uncovered, he washes them, causing less pain than expected.

"Now we need to get you out of that shirt without hurting you too much."

A chill of distress sweeps over. Other than the linens over her wounds, she's otherwise naked underneath the borrowed clothing. Luke assists her in pulling her arms inside each sleeve and lifts the shirt over her head. Her breasts are the only flesh newly exposed as most of her torso is covered in bandages. Her nipples pucker at the change in temperature.

For a few moments, she's too embarrassed to meet his eyes, to see him looking at her. The way he goes to work removing the soiled coverings and cleaning her cuts with nothing but care and professionalism on his face helps set her more at ease.

Knowing her upper chest and belly would be similar to her arms did nothing to prepare her for the horrific sight. She doesn't want to see, but she can't look away. Only the part of her breasts that had been covered by her bra had been spared. The extent and closeness of the markings resemble the wounds of a severe fire victim. The only way she could be more disfigured is if the kidnapper had burned her.

Tears flow down her face and drop from her chin. He notices and rushes to retrieve tissues.

With fast and efficient movements, he cleans and tends to her upper body, his hands and eyes never lingering anywhere that would make her uncomfortable. Applying the fresh gauze takes the longest. After an eternity of feeling exposed, he slips a clean t-shirt over her head and helps her arms into the sleeves. A sigh of relief escapes her even though she knows he's only halfway finished.

Luke slides down the too-big sweatpants that barely remain over her hips and tucks some of the sheet over her pelvis and under her thighs, helping Sandra retain some dignity.

When he removes the covering over her left thigh, she sees the stab wound has been expertly stitched. He touches his hands to both sides of the gash.

"This is healing well," he reassures her when he notices her watching him. "Nothing's abnormally warm. I think we avoided an infection."

Sandra feels a little color on her cheeks. "Only because someone did such a good job of patching me up."

Days ago, she'd been afraid of dying at the hands of her kidnapper. When he had left her in the woods, she'd been too tired and relieved to consider what dying there would be like. Now she wonders if shock, dehydration, infection, or animals would have killed her first. She shudders.

"You okay?"

"Yeah." She realizes she's gripping the sheets and forces her fingers to relax.

Once her legs are unwrapped, he cleans the entirety of her lower half and smooths an oil on her ankle.

"What's? That?"

"It's arnica. It's great for muscle aches and bruises."

"You. Have. Every. Thing."

"I go through a lot of this myself. It's great after a long day of splitting wood." He gets up and washes the oil from his hands before coming back to wrap up her legs. With care, he pulls fresh sweatpants over them.

"There." A broad smile widens his lips as if he's admiring a job well done. Then he looks up at her face. "Just one thing left."

She raises her eyebrows in question.

"I'm going to brush and attempt to braid your hair. I had a little sister once. Maybe I can remember how." He retrieves his comb from the bathroom and cuts a length of twine from a spool in the closet.

No one has combed or brushed her hair in years, and she relaxes and enjoys the experience, even as he works out the knots.

"Well," he says after he secures the braid with twine, "if you squint at it, then it's passible as 'not too bad'."

She titters. "Thank you."

"Don't mention it. Now, I'm going to be outside for a couple of hours. Bear still hasn't figured out how to chop wood. You should rest, but would you like to have a book nearby in case you don't sleep the whole time?"

"Yes. Please."

Luke brings another basket out of a closet and over to the bed.

She marvels at how organized everything is. Probably due to his military training.

"I've got something in here for everyone, I think. Each month, I send off the ones I've read."

Inside is a wide range of books from classics by Shakespeare and Jane Austin to current crime thrillers and romances. She selects Pride and Prejudice; it'll be an easy and fun reread for her.

He helps her get comfortable and puts a glass of water within reach.

"Alright, don't worry. I won't be far, and no one comes anywhere near here anyway." He leaves her to nap and read.

* * *

When Luke shuts off the cabin lights for the night, and the room is only lit by the soft glow of the fire, Sandra finds it difficult to close her eyes. Whenever she does, her hearing heightens like it was when her head was trapped beneath that awful hood for so long. Every nighttime creak or whooshing of the wind quickens her pulse.

She lays awake listening for the sound of footsteps coming toward her. In her current stage of healing and being unable to walk, she's helpless and defenseless.

Each time she drifts off into a restless sleep, there's always the chance of continuing the nightmare she lived through. The monster who tortured her surely had a myriad of other ghastly ideas in his imagination to inflict upon her or others. Her creativity runs wild when she sleeps imagining fresh horrors.

One question continues to plague her above everything else: Why did he let her go?

Was it only so she could die alone in the woods? Why didn't he just kill her?

What if he discovers she's still alive?

Her muscles twitch as her body relaxes into sleep, but her mind conjures sensations of being restrained again. This time, Sandra finds herself able to look down and see her bindings. Her body is secured in metal strands of barbed wire. The more she struggles, the more the cruel barbs tear her skin and make her bleed.

The monster stands over her, his face dark and unrecognizable. She thought he'd laugh and gloat over her torment, but he never makes a sound. He could be anybody. Sandra never saw any part of him. The only noises he ever made were footsteps and breathing.

She squirms and writhes against the wire, trying to get away, but once again she's helpless and within his grasp. She tries to scream, but no noise comes out.

His hand appears holding an old hook this time. Slowly, he scrapes it over her skin, teasing her with it. Her body tenses under the cold steel. He plunges it deep into her belly, tearing her open. She stares, slack-jawed, as he shreds her skin and spills out her intestines.

For the first time ever, he speaks. "Sandra."

She's shocked he knows her name. "Who are you?" she whispers weakly.

His face begins to come into focus as he leans closer. "It's me. Luke."

She blinks, startling back to reality and realizing she'd been dreaming. Luke sits next to her on the bed.

"You were having a nightmare." His voice is weighed with concern.

Her eyes begin to tear up in a mixture of horror and relief.

"Luke, it was so awful," she moans.

"I know." He takes her hand in both of his; a thumb gently strokes her skin. "It's over now. It was just a dream."

His touch comforts her. Keeping track of the days is difficult, but she estimates he's been taking care of her, doing everything for her, for well over a week. Not once has he made her feel uneasy or been unkind.

"Do you want me to stay with you until you fall back asleep?" he offers.

Sandra mulls it over. After the nightmare, she doesn't want to be alone, even though the couch he sleeps on isn't more than a few feet away. Though it's strange to admit, Luke's presence makes her feel safe. That's something she's craving more of right now.

Movement at the door stops her heart and jerks her eyes in that direction. The glow from the firelight dances on the wood.

Still, the thought nags her. *It could have been him. Did he go back to where he left me? Is he looking for me? Please, God, don't let him find me.*

"What if–?" She pauses, a touch of self-consciousness tugs at her, making her not want to continue her request. But she might not be able to sleep now, if she doesn't.

"Yes? Go on."

"What if you stayed with me? Just for tonight?" She bites her lip, but the words are out now and can't be taken back.

"Like, sleep on the bed next to you, stay with you?"

She nods, while her cheeks ignite another burn–their new permanent state with him.

"Sure. I can do that." He gets up, walks around to the empty half of the mattress, and slides under the covers. He takes her near hand into his, but, always a gentleman, keeps his body a respectful distance away.

She stares into his eyes which are now level with hers. "Maybe a little bit closer," she whispers. A rush surges through her at this proximity, but she longs for more of his heat.

He moves an inch or two towards her. For a moment, she's unsure how to respond, until a slight grin appears on his face.

Feeling a tad more confident, she repeats one word. "Closer."

He inches again.

She smiles and laughs, and the playful game continues until his arm is around her, and her shoulder presses against his bare chest. His slow steady breathing so close to her ear relaxes and soothes her. Soon, Sandra drifts off into a peaceful sleep.

* * *

"The end." Luke closes the book on his lap with a soft thud.

Sandra leans back against the headboard and sighs contentedly. "It's such a good book."

"Mhm," he agrees.

"Even the fourth time through."

"That was your fourth time?" His eyes widen.

Sandra grins. "Yeah. I'm an addict. What can I say?" She sits up, remembering something. "Does this mean we can watch the movie tonight?"

"Absolutely." He gets up and walks to the pantry, talking to her over his shoulder. "I think we can even do it right."

"Right? Is there a wrong way to watch a movie?"

"Of course there is." Luke turns back triumphantly to hold up two bags of microwavable popcorn. "Without popcorn."

Sandra laughs. "Good thinking."

He plops the bags down on the counter. "We'll watch it right after dinner, okay?"

"I can't wait. Hey, I'd like to help with dinner tonight. There must be something I can do."

Sandra was slowly making progress with doing things for herself. Luke had fashioned her a crutch out of wood from his outdoor shop, and she'd been able to get to the bathroom on her own yesterday. He'd stayed close and, of course, doted on her every step of the way. Her ankle was still pretty tender, but he made sure it was wrapped well before she attempted her trek and reassured her a little weight on it wouldn't do any lasting damage.

"I think I can find something you can help with that'll be easy on you." He picks up a small legal pad. The front page has a list of items scrawled across the blue lines. He touches a pen to the paper but sets them both down without writing anything, a disappointed look on his face.

"What? What's wrong?"

He sighs and scrubs his face with his hands before turning and meeting her gaze mournfully. "It's just that, I was going to add popcorn to my shopping list, but you won't be here when I get more. I've had that three-pack for months now and have only had one so far. I don't often eat it when I'm by myself. It's been nice to have some company, but I know you're probably eager to get back to your friends and family."

Sandra frowns. She can't imagine what it's been like for him to be out here all alone for so long. He's such a genuinely kind person; it's a shame he's tucked away from society.

"Bear no doubt wishes I'd eat more popcorn." He laughs. "I give him half of it when I do." After another deep breath, he adds, "I'm really going to miss you."

She can't believe her luck. How did she finally meet an amazing man who reads to her, cooks for her, massages her feet, who she could actually see herself enjoying dating, only to get to spend four weeks with and never see again?

It's not fair.

"Do you think I could visit you? After?"

He shakes his head with a pursed forehead and lips. "No. They'll blindfold you so you can't find your way back. We'll never meet again after you leave."

Her heart pounds in terror at the mention of the blindfold. They'll need to sedate her, or she'll have a panic attack.

"Are you okay?" He touches her shoulder and snaps her back to the present.

"Yeah. Just having a daymare." She wants to tell him she'll miss him, too, but she doesn't want to come across as corny and desperate. Even the nice guys don't like that.

She weighs her options: regret leaving him for the rest of her life or ask him if she can stay. The fact she thought of staying surprises her. Her stomach flips and somersaults. In two weeks, she needs to decide whether to broach the subject and change her life forever. Hell, either way, her life will never be the same after what she's been through after being kidnapped.

Eager to think of something else, she asks with a laugh, "What time is dinner?"

He smiles at her enthusiasm for the movie. They had finished breakfast barely an hour ago.

"Let me get some things done, and we can have an early dinner tonight."

"Yay!"

11

Falling

Sandra spends the morning reading and the early afternoon taking a sponge bath. The stab wound on her thigh is the only part of her that still requires a covering besides the binding on her ankle. After some light begging, he had shown her how to bandage and wrap both areas on her own.

It was nice to be able to start doing things for herself. And it was nice to be able to bathe herself again. Luke never made it weird, but it was still uncomfortable, especially since they weren't having physical relations.

Yet.

As she dries off and gets dressed, her mind wonders what it would be like to have sex with him. Is he the perfect gentleman in bed as he is out of it? Her body flushes and tingles while she's thinking about it.

No guy has ever made her feel this way. It's like he came right out of a romance movie and into her life.

Sandra looks around the cabin. It's small but cozy. Maybe they could build an addition to make more room. If she stayed. If he even wanted her to. So many ifs.

She shakes her head.

Once dressed, she uses her crutch to hobble to the door and step out onto the covered porch.

The light squeal of the door swinging shut, draws his attention. Luke glances up with a smile and waves at her. She waves back.

He's on his knees weeding the garden by hand, his torso bare to soak up the sun's rays. Sandra takes a seat in the single wooden chair on the porch and watches, admiring his body. When he's done, he comes to the bottom of the steps.

"I'm going to go forage for our dinner salad. Do you need anything first?"

"Nope. I'm great."

"Good. I'll see you in a few. Come on, Bear." From a post that holds his shirt, he grabs a burlap messenger bag and swings the strap over his shoulder. Whistling, he walks into the woods followed by his massive dog.

He's gone for maybe half an hour. Sandra spends most of the time enjoying the fresh air.

But every snapping twig beyond the clearing of the yard sends her heart into a racing frenzy. What if *he's* out there? What if he creeps up behind Luke while he's selecting only the ripest fruits and stabs him in the back? And then he comes for her.

The next figure she sees will be someone she doesn't recognize. A tall, strong stranger, striding with purpose toward her. Only this time, he's ready to finish what he started. There is no escape.

She waits with shallow breaths. The air tickles her arm hairs which stand on end like someone's watching her. Not even the warm rays of the sun, low enough to peek below the awning of the porch can warm until Luke returns.

And then, finally, he does.

A sigh escapes her at the sight of his handsome, yet rugged face. Bear trots with raised, wagging tail at his side.

She follows him inside and sits on the bed while he proudly shows off his acquisitions. Almost every day, he introduces her to something new to eat from the forest, often things she's never heard of or noticed before.

I want to learn to forage with him.

Tonight, he brought back dandelion greens, chickweed, miner's lettuce, and clover for their salad as well as morels, oyster mushrooms, and fiddleheads to saute with butter and garlic.

"I found a meadow with so many dandelions. I plan to go back tomorrow to gather a bunch and make dandelion wine."

Sandra doesn't know how long it takes to make dandelion wine, but she can't imagine it's less than two weeks.

"I've never had dandelion wine." Her voice catches, and she drops her head.

"What?" His brows jut up for his hairline. "We'll remedy that. I have at least a bottle or two left out in the shed. We can have some with dinner."

"That sounds lovely."

He lets her prepare the salad while he sautees the vegetables and venison steak. Even the berry vinaigrette dressing came from foraged produce.

The meal looks and smells amazing, as always, and makes her mouth water in anticipation. He moves the dining chair out to the porch, and they eat it in the cooling air as the sun goes down.

When they're finished, he takes the chair back inside so she can dry the dishes as he washes them.

We're like the perfect little couple already. It could be like this every day if I stay.

Sandra's glad when the chores are done because she needs the distraction of the movie to get her mind off these crazy thoughts.

The television is anchored to a beam that divides the cabin in half. It's obvious that it's primarily watched from the bed.

Sandra settles herself on the bed while Luke readies the movie. Then he comes and sits on the nearby dining chair.

"There's plenty of room." She pats the bed next to her.

His eyes tentatively meet hers, and her heart skips a beat. "Are you sure?"

"I am."

With a soft smile that makes her melt, he stands and walks around the bed to climb up near to her.

"I don't bite," she says when leaves too much room in the middle. He scoots a little closer, and she closes most of the rest of the gap so their elbows brush.

When the movie finishes, Sandra wipes a tear from her eye, and gasps when she remembers, "We didn't have the popcorn."

"Oh no. I wasn't hungry after dinner and forgot about it."

"Same. We could have some now?"

"We should watch a second one then. You pick while I go make it." He sets his box of current movies on the bed for her to choose from.

"Can you stand another romance?"

"What do you have in mind?"

Sandra holds up "When Harry Met Sally".

"Ah. A classic. I'm always up for that one."

They watch the movie and eat their popcorn sitting closer together this time. Sandra ends up falling asleep with her head on his shoulder.

* * *

She wakes up to him moving her to a lying down position and is grateful she won't wake up in the morning with a kink in her neck.

"I missed the end of the movie."

"We can watch it again. You need sleep so your body can heal." His voice is low and soothing in the dim light.

She relishes him tucking her in and realizes she'll never tire of him taking care of her. As his hands pull away, she reaches out and grabs one. Their eyes meet.

"Would you stay? Sleep next to me?" Her heart races, wondering what he'll say, if she's being too desperate or a burden. "Just so I don't have nightmares?"

"Yeah. Of course. Let me check the fire first." His bare feet pad across the hardwood floor.

Sandra turns towards the empty side of the bed in anticipation. Her heart hasn't slowed, and now her stomach is all atwitter. She'll be the first to admit she's never been in love. Once in freshman year, she had a crush on a boy on the football team; but like most jocks, he only had eyes for the cheerleaders. Sandra was way too clumsy to be a cheerleader.

Is this love? If yes, how can she dampen the burning desire that he never leaves her side again?

Finally, he slides into the bed across from her. She can't take her eyes off him. She reaches out, and he interlocks his fingers with hers. Electric shivers at his touch race up her arm and through her body. His face is only a foot away. Her eyes leave his to creep down and linger over his lips. She blushes when she realizes she just licked her own.

"Luke?" The word is barely audible as she wars within herself over bringing a voice to her desire.

"Yes?"

He might as well have said "I do" with the way the softness of his response warms her. It was definitely safe to make her request.

"Would you kiss me?" The words tumble out. If she'd taken her time she might have lost her nerve. She's never asked someone this before. She's never desired a kiss so desperately until he came along.

His mouth falls open with a surprised expression that twinkles in his eyes. "Kiss you? Are you sure?"

Her body trembles in anticipation. She nods in assent.

"Oh my God, Sandra, I want to kiss you so badly." He lifts her hand and presses his lips to it. The gesture gives her goosebumps. "I just didn't want to kiss you if you didn't want it and come across as the desperate bachelor hermit."

They share a giggle which dies as he scoots closer. The tightness in her chest and the racing of her heart are almost painful. No doubt exists in her mind that he's anything but the most amazing kisser.

He inches toward her tentatively, as if he's giving her time to withdraw her request if she doesn't really mean it. She leans in instead, her lips parting. Their skin meets. It would take her breath away if she wasn't holding it in anticipation. His hand releases hers and slips around her waist, drawing her body nearer to his.

Sandra's whole body aches for more. She presses her lips more firmly on his. His tongue teases the opening of her mouth. She parts her lips, the encouragement is rewarded by his tongue filling her mouth.

Her arms find their way around him and pull their bodies

closer. Luke leans over her, careful to not put his weight anywhere that would cause her pain.

A moan escapes her.

He pulls back.

She tries not to be embarrassed.

"I'm sorry. Did I hurt you?" Concern creases his forehead.

She's flushed and breathless. "No. It was wonderful."

"I don't want to go too fast or make you think I'm taking advantage."

Sandra nods, missing the warmth of his mouth on hers.

He lays down again. "May I hold you while you sleep?"

"Yes. I would like that." She drifts to sleep tucked in his arms.

* * *

Sandra has never slept as well as she does that night. When she wakes up, she can barely believe that Luke's arms are around her.

"Good morning, beautiful," he whispers when their eyes meet.

"How long have you been watching me sleep?"

"Only a few minutes. I haven't been awake long." He kisses her forehead, and her skin tingles. "Shall I start us some coffee?"

"Wait." She grabs his arm. "Can we stay like this a little bit longer?"

"Sure. Whatever you want." He relaxes next to her again.

She lays there thinking, stroking his arm. He leans his head against hers.

"Luke?"

"Hmm?"

"How long until your –,' she pauses, trying to recall what he had referred to his monthly delivery person as, and comes up short, "shopper guy comes back?"

He laughs. "My handler? Let's see. Today's the thirteenth. He comes on the twenty-fifth of each month, so twelve days? Why are you asking?"

Sandra can't stop the tears that well up in her eyes nor the quiet sobs that lodge in her throat. She turns and buries her head in his chest, and he squeezes her.

"What's wrong? Did I do something?"

"No." She shakes her head and grips his arm.

"Hey. It's okay. What's going on?"

She tilts her head back so she can see him. His forehead wrinkles with worry; his eyes search her face for answers. She remembers the sweet taste and passion of last night's kiss.

"I-." This is it. Is she really going to say it? Does she mean it? It's not a commitment; it's just voicing a desire. A knot twists and aches in her core. If she doesn't bring it up, they can't talk about it. What if he doesn't want it, too?

Here goes nothing. And maybe everything.

"What if I don't want to leave–you?" She swallows hard and holds her breath.

His eyes get wide. She can't tell which way he's leaning.

"You mean, like–." He licks his lips. "Stay? With me?"

"Yeah."

The clock ticks slower as she waits for an answer.

For a moment, they stare at each other.

She wonders if he's evaluating her as a companion. *Am I too needy?* For the two weeks prior, she's required a lot of his care and attention. Granted, it wouldn't always be that way. She's starting to get around better on her own. She's trying to lessen his responsibility.

Just as her fear that he'll say no and reject her offer grows to a suffocating level, he leans in and presses his lips to hers. This kiss is much more full of need than the one last night. His tongue greedily fills her mouth. He pulls her hips to his and slides over her, careful to not put too much weight on her.

She runs her hands up his arms searching for access to more of his skin. They glide down and grab the bottom of his shirt to tug it up his chiseled torso. The two of them separate long enough for him to pull his t-shirt over his head. As quickly as they can, their tongues intertwine again.

An ache grows between her legs. If he pursues it in the slightest, she's willing to have sex with him. Sex seems like such a crude word for it, especially with Luke. Will this be the first time she makes love to someone? It might not be love, but she's never felt this deep affection and desire for anyone before.

She pulls him to her, wanting him pressed against her. She grips at him, relishing his warm skin and muscular form.

He's gentle and controlled in response, remembering her wounds and respecting her body. His calloused hands knead down her back to her waist but go no further. He caresses a trail up her side, making her breasts hunger for more attention.

He's being too chivalrous with his touches, and she wants to tell him he won't break her. She's ready.

Sandra grabs his hand and moves it to her chest, arching to meet his touch.

His palm begins to press against it but instead jerks back. He sits up, his face flushed.

Sandra takes a gulp of air to regain her composure and searches for an answer to her confusion. "What's wrong?"

"I can't." He covers his face with his hands.

She sits up and squeezes his hands in hers. "Talk to me."

When his eyes meet hers, her heart breaks. His eyes shine with care.

He shakes his head with despair. "You don't understand, Sandra."

The soft way her name falls from his mouth makes her swoon.

With a deep sigh, he looks away into the cabin. "It can get so lonely out here. You'd have to give up everyone you ever knew to remain with me."

It's agonizing for her when their eyes meet again.

"You must have family, friends, people who miss you. People you miss." His voice trails off.

Sandra's vision blurs as tears fill her eyes.

"You would never be able to talk to them again. It would be as if you disappeared."

She nods. She had considered this, the finality of the decision. Her friends. Her parents. Her cat.

"All that being said, if we make our relationship physical, it would be even more painful for me if–when–you leave."

Sandra swallows the lump in her throat. "And if I want to stay?"

"I would love that. I mean, I love–." His face lights up, his voice filled with excitement. He catches himself from finishing his sentence.

When he's subdued, he repeats, "I would love that." He holds up one finger. "But. Would you think about it? Like, think long and hard about it? For, let's say, two days? If in two days, you still want to stay, we'll have a serious discussion about it."

This seems like a reasonable ask. "Agreed."

He brings one of her hands to his mouth and presses it to his lips. "You are a very special person, Cassandra."

* * *

Sandra didn't take his plea for her to think about it lightly. For the next two days, dissecting the decision became an obsession.

At her request to help keep the nightmares away, he sleeps next to her. She wakes in the morning in his warm embrace. He kisses her forehead 'good morning'.

They begin to do things jointly like an old married couple as her wounds heal and she becomes more mobile. They make every meal and clean up afterward together. She sits outside on the porch in the afternoons while he gardens or chops wood. In the evenings, they curl up in bed and watch a movie. He massages her legs to help their circulation until she can be more active. They start reading another book together.

If this isn't the perfect existence, then Sandra wonders what is. Her whole body fills with unruly butterflies each time their eyes meet.

What if this is love, and I let it go?

If she left, she'd have to endure being blindfolded and driven away. Once she gets in that car, she won't be able to change her mind. The handler would drive her to a hospital. After the doctors examine her and find her to be healing well from Luke's amazing care, she would be released to her family. Her parents and friends would be overjoyed to have her back.

The police would make her recount the torture she endured. Maybe they would catch the guy, and he wouldn't be able to do this to anyone else.

But she never saw his face. She wouldn't be able to pick him out of a line-up. On the chance that they apprehended him through forensic evidence, like traces of her urine in the back of his van, she would have to testify and tell her story again on the stand.

The monster is too careful for that, though. They'll never find out who he was. She hadn't even heard his voice.

All this would be painful, yes. But what if it paled in comparison to the pain she felt by leaving the love of her life all alone in the woods to live out the rest of his days missing her?

What if she met another guy and settled for him because she let Luke slip away? What if every night when they made love, she saw Luke's face instead of her husband's? What if they had kids, and she couldn't help but wonder what her and Luke's children would have looked like every time she saw them? She could grow old and never truly be present with her family because she was stuck on the one she abandoned out in the woods.

What if they forced Luke to relocate because of her? He's built himself quite the homestead. It would be cruel for him to have to leave his home, even if it was a lonely one.

And what if she tried to come back and find him? And couldn't?

All these questions eat away at her during every quiet moment. She lies awake at night listening to his soft breathing, wondering if she could handle never seeing his face again.

What sort of hell would her life become? Pining for the one she let go. Going through all the trauma and torture to abandon her chance at true happiness.

No one had ever made her feel special and cared for the way he did.

* * *

The second evening since he'd asked her to think about it, Sandra sits in the Adirondack chair on the porch. Luke's in the yard, measuring and sawing lumber for a new woodworking project. She knows he moved his equipment out of the shed so they could be closer while he worked.

As the light fades from the sky, he packs up his tools and sawhorses and puts them away. When he walks up the few steps to her, she asks, "What are you making?"

"Another chair like that." He points to the one she's in.

"Oh?" Is he banking on her saying she'll stay?

"Yeah. I'm memorizing the way you look sitting there so when you're gone, I can look over and picture you next to me."

"About that." She stands up so her face is closer to his. "I think I've reached a decision."

"Okay."

She takes a step towards him, her eyes searching his, wondering what answer from her he wants more. He's been living alone for so long; maybe he doesn't want a full-time companion. Maybe his dog is enough.

Who are you kidding? That's ridiculous, Sandra. Everyone needs more than just a dog.

Is he desperate for her because she's been his only human contact in years? Someone as kind and gentle as Luke has to need to be around other people. It's a wonder he hasn't gone insane already. All things considered, he's shockingly normal.

Sandra takes another step. Their bodies are inches apart. She places a hand on his chest. His throat works with a hard swallow.

"Luke." She examines his face for any sign to give her confidence or pause. He's unreadable. "I thought about it as you asked me to."

He nods, his breathing shallow.

"And-." Her eyes well up with tears. She didn't want to get emotional about this and ruin the moment.

He puts a hand on either side of her face. "Sandra. Whatever your decision is, just know that it's okay."

She sniffs and breathes to collect herself. He's giving her permission to stay or to leave. She knows he desires her to reach a conclusion on her own so she can live with it. Of course, he can't tell her how much he'll miss her if she leaves. And he can't tell her if he wants her to stay. The decision belongs solely to her.

She wipes her eyes and looks up into his. "I want to stay."

At first, his expression doesn't change. Then, as the words sink in, his eyes widen. His hands press against her face.

"Are you sure?"

"Yes. I imagined my life without you, and no part of me wants to lose you." Her body trembles with the suspense of waiting for him to reveal his emotions one way or another.

His eyes dart back and forth, scrutinizing her face.

"Cassandra."

Her knees weaken at the way her name sounds coming from his mouth. She needs a response.

"My love."

Then his lips are on hers taking her breath away. His tongue invades her mouth and dances with hers.

Oh my god, he called me his love! For the first time ever, she loves and is loved in return. Her body burns with desire for him. She presses closer to his warmth.

He pulls away abruptly, making her wonder if she's done something wrong. Before she can ask, he speaks. "What if we make tonight special? Like a date?" He strokes her hair.

She smiles. She would have gone to bed with him right now, but the delay will make it all the more enjoyable. A date with Luke sounds like the best night of her life. "Yes."

His eyes widen and sparkle with delight. "I have emergency candles on hand. We'll light those and eat by candlelight. I have a homemade triple berry mead that will go lovely with a steak."

She nods her head as he talks, affirming everything he's saying sounds delightful.

"I have a funny request." A sheepish grin plays on his lips.

"Do tell."

"I've always wanted to carry my girl across the threshold."

A flutter within prompts a shy laugh from her.

"May I?" He holds out his hands.

"Yes." Sandra finds herself at a loss for more than single syllables. A mix of lust, love, desire, and ecstasy swirls inside her. This is everything she's ever wanted in life. Who knew she would find her Casanova in the middle of nowhere? Casanova and Cassandra. It has a great ring to it.

He dips down and scoops her up as if she weighs nothing. When he approaches the door, she unlatches it for them, and he carries her inside.

The evening is as wonderful as she imagined it would be. After dinner, he puts an Eric Clapton record on the player and slow dances with her. They only last a few songs before finding themselves naked under the sheets in a climaxing conclusion to the best night of her life.

12

Back in the Tree

A strange, soft pattering she can't place rouses Sandra. Leaning back, she swivels her head from one side to the other looking for where it's coming from. In the dim light of early morning, she catches a glimpse of Luke out of the corner of her eye. He's standing off to the side in a wide-legged stance men use when they're peeing.

She needs to pee as well. Her bladder is painfully full. The tender skin of her chest, breasts, and stomach, which has been mercilessly scratched by the bark all night long, captures her attention with its complaints. Still, she's grateful to the tree for keeping her safe from the wolves through the night.

The sight of Luke brings to mind the darkness over her head as he kicked her, electrocuted her, hung her, and carved in her flesh. Hot tears fill her eyes. Her chest tightens. How could someone be so cruel?

The real cruelty was what came after all the torture. He made her trust him. He made her *love* him.

She sniffs in order to breathe, and the sound is louder in the quiet woods than she intended.

"The little birdie is awake, Bear." His voice is no longer soft and soothing but rough and gloating. How is he the same person she so recently made love to?

The tears pour down her face as the gravity of the betrayal hits her. He was the only one besides her parents and best friend that she ever fully trusted. After the trauma, she gave herself to him. And it was set up from the beginning.

"Good morning, Sandra." He stands a few feet beneath her looking up with a pleased grin on his face. "Are you coming down for breakfast?"

Down? Hell no. She doesn't want to know what he'll do to her if she does.

An ache builds in her throat. Her nose continues to congest. She turns her face away. All the vile words she has for him will never be enough.

A crackling noise sounds behind her. He must be getting the fire going again.

Think, Sandra, think. She presses her face against the tree. *You can't just sit here all day.* What else is there to do? She can't outrun him. The only reason she got as far as she did is that he didn't initially chase her. He was willing to let her get eaten by the wolves before he caught up with her.

She critically examines every word he said, everything he did over the last four weeks. There had been no way for her to know what he was. He was good. He had practice doing this.

"How many others were there?" Her voice chokes in her throat.

"Come again?" His casual tone is so like the Luke she fell in love with but devoid of warmth or empathy.

"How many other women have you kidnapped and killed?" She forces her words to carry this time.

"Oh, I haven't killed anyone." His answer's dismissive.

"What?" Her forehead creases in bewilderment. A hint of hope sprouts within her.

"Yeah. You might find that hard to believe, but I've never taken anyone's life."

Her mind takes a minute to process this information. It doesn't make sense. A piece of the truth is missing.

A delicious smell teases her nose. He's cooking sausage or something similar over the fire. Her stomach growls and rolls with desire.

"Then what?" Her words are quiet, not necessarily meant for him to hear. In her confusion, she doesn't know what to ask.

"I didn't kill them. They committed suicide."

He's insane. Truly insane.

Wishing she could shut out this whole situation and wake up in her warm bed, Sandra shuts her eyes. Her pelvis and tailbone hurt from sitting with a tree branch between her legs all night long.

She can't believe she had him between her legs hours ago. They'd made love so many times over the past several days. She'd even told him she would stay and live with him in the woods. How could she have been so manipulated? Reminding herself that he's practiced this with other women before her does little to comfort her.

"Are you coming down and having breakfast? The coffee's hot."

Coffee. The thought of the warm, comforting beverage tempts her, but only a little. The memories of coffee with him are drowned out by his psychopathy.

She shakes her head. Why would she willingly come down and be near him? Still, her curiosity wins. "What will you do to me if I do?"

"There's really no telling, but I've got a list of ideas." He sounds amused, entertained.

Prick.

"You aren't going to let me go, are you?" Her stomach tightens into knots bracing for the answer she expects and receives.

He lets out a big, hearty laugh. "That's a good one, Sandra."

"Why?" As soon as it exits her lips, she knows the question is a dumb one, but she can't help herself. Hot tears sting her eyes. She's grasping for any thread of hope and coming up empty.

"Because that's not how the game works." He clicks his tongue like she's the foolish one.

"What game? I don't want to play a game." She adjusts her position to take the pressure off her tailbone. The leaves rustle around her, perking up Bear's ears.

"Once I choose someone to play my game, it only ends one way."

"What made you pick me?"

"You were so boring and predictable. I figured you needed something to spice up your life. With the movies you watched and the books you read, I recognized you as one of those hopeless romantics who would fall for my sad little story."

Her cheeks burn. Was she truly *that* predictable?

She knows better than to ask how it ends. The answer is obvious. "When did you put out the ski mask?"

"Yesterday at lunch. I knew you were going to do the math and realize my handler should arrive today." The mirth in his voice is apparent.

"Is anything you said real?"

"Hmm. Let's see. I do live alone with Bear. That was real. The rest of it? All made up." The self-satisfaction in his voice is clear. She can imagine the grin on his face.

The pressure of the branch between her legs reaches an unbearable ache. Using her bra around the tree trunk as leverage to help her, she stands up. With slow, planned movements, she brings up a leg and gets it under her. From there, getting to her feet is fairly easy. Without jeopardizing her balance, she begins stretching what she can. Her joints pop with satisfying relief.

"Look at that lovely ass you have." He lets out a few low, appreciative moans. "I doubt you're going to let me tap that again."

"Creep," she whispers, not wanting to give him the pleasure of a response. Now that her butt has some relief, her attention goes back to her full bladder. Taking her panties off while standing on the branch sounds too difficult. He'd probably enjoy the show, too. Not that he isn't getting one and enjoying it now. This is what he'd planned on all along.

She remembers soiling herself when he tased her a month ago. Is she really going to start and end this nightmare with pissed panties?

Her bladder is screaming. She doesn't have much of a choice. Steadying against the tree trunk, Sandra releases one of the bra straps to use that hand to pull the front of her panties to the side. She tucks her tailbone and allows herself to pee. The urine sprays out before her in a strong stream, leaving her mostly dry until the end when it becomes a dribble and runs down her legs.

At least my underpants aren't soaked.

* * *

The morning passes at a painfully slow pace. Every muscle in her body hurts from being tense in one way or another. Now that her bladder's relieved, her parched mouth and insides beg for a drink. Her throat's dry and her lips are chapped. The skin on her face, hands, and chest is chafed and raw from pressing against the bark for hours.

Many times, she considered trying to run for it when he wasn't paying attention, but she doesn't have a clue which way to go. She'd rather he shoot her than get torn apart by wolves, but it doesn't sound as if he will outright kill her. If she runs, he might wound her to make it easier for the wolves. She tries to swallow the hard lump in her throat.

"Don't you have anything better to do?"

He'd spent the day reading, chopping wood, and drinking tea he prepared over the fire from fir needles, like this is some little camping trip.

"Like what? What could be more important than babysitting my little birdie?"

"Like a job? A hobby?"

"Heh, heh, heh." His laugh is maniacal. "This is my *job*. This is what I do, how I make money, and my favorite pastime. Each time is different from the last. I invented the game years ago. Initially, I thought it was going to be a one-time thing. I spent months planning and picking my perfect first player. Wanting to capture every moment, I filmed it so I could watch it over and over again. Then I stumbled upon an online community of like-minded individuals and realized others would enjoy watching me play my game. When I shared my footage with them, they were in awe of my artistry and willing to pay a hefty price to keep viewing my content."

Several minutes pass before the realization of what he's saying fully sinks in.

"You're recording me?"

"I've been recording you the whole time, my dear. All of it. Kidnapping you. Torturing you. Making love to you. You sleeping in my bed. I recorded you pissing from a tree branch a couple of hours ago."

Her stomach lurches with disgust as his words settle in. "And you post it on the internet?" She feels ill. Will her family or friends stumble upon it in their search for her?

"Yes, and make a considerable amount of money doing so. Then I find another contestant, and the game starts again."

"Aren't you afraid you'll get caught?"

"I'm much too smart for that" He waves his hand in a scoffing manner. "I take the footage, edit myself out, modify my voice, and no one knows what I look or sound like. By the time it's posted, I've moved on from the area."

She squeezes her eyes shut in a mix of disgust and humiliation, not wanting to converse with him further.

The day drags on into the afternoon. The air becomes warm and lulls her into a restless doze. She's dreaming of lying by a beach, drinking a Mai Tai, when pain assaults her foot. The outer edge of her foot is dull, throbbing agony while a searing knife of torture shoots up her leg.

She screams, making her throat feel as if it's on fire, and instinctually yanks her foot up, barely keeping her balance on the branch.

Sandra stares down in disbelief, her eyes unwilling at first to process the abnormality. The two smallest toes on her left foot have been lopped off. Blood pours from the wound. She clutches it, trying to stop the flow. Her fingers slip and slide. Something beneath her catches her eye even amid her suffering.

Luke stands at the base of the tree holding a hatchet, a sadistic grin on his blood-spattered face, looking up at her with glee.

* * *

When Sandra initially chose her place on the tree, her main thought was to be out of the reach of a wolf's teeth. She hadn't considered she needed to be past the range of Luke's abilities as well.

By standing on a root that stuck up from the base of the tree, and extending his arm, he had just been able to reach her foot with the hatchet.

Tears pouring down her face mercifully blur the sight of him. Her balance is precarious. With much effort, she hops and turns around until she can lean against the tree and have a better hold on her mutilated, bleeding foot.

The blood gushes out in streams and spurts. She knows she needs to stop it, her human nature makes her want to fight for survival and not just give up. All she has are her pee-dribbled panties and her bra that now hangs off one shoulder.

As her tears begin to clear, she glances down and sees him holding a small sports camera. He must be zooming in so his future audience can get a good look at her sitting in only her underpants in the tree, her hands smeared with blood.

If she gets up now and takes off her panties to ebb the flow, it will just increase his satisfaction. Is that what he wants? To get her naked again? She looks into the camera and then into his demonic eyes and shakes her head. She's done playing.

Escape isn't an option. Even if there was a way to get away from him now, she can't get far on a mangled foot. The scent of blood will bring out the wolves soon anyway. Nightfall is only hours away.

She glances at the branches above her. They'll support her weight for quite a while. With all the determination she can muster, she gingerly stands up and starts to climb. Each step of her injured foot grasping a tree branch is agony. Many times, she cries out in pain.

Every flex of that foot causes her to lose more blood. The world spins as her head becomes woozy with the loss of vital fluid. Her entire leg pulses and throbs.

She refuses to look down.

Up and up she climbs until the branches begin to thin and bow under her. Here she settles, spacing her weight across several that are close together.

She knows Luke must have watched her and recorded every second. Was he pleased? She tries to push thoughts of him from her mind. The limbs between them mostly hide her up here.

Her aching foot screams for attention. Now that she's mostly out of his sight, she's willing to remove her panties and try to ebb the flow. She cries out again as she presses them over her open flesh and winds her bra around to secure them in place. Both garments quickly dampen with crimson.

She leans against the tree to catch her breath.

From up here, she can see the sun. She watches it in a daze of pain as it moves over the forest toward the horizon.

Gradually, her surroundings darken as the golden orb sets. The wolves begin to howl. The sound doesn't hold as much terror for her as it did last night. She knows they'll be drawn to the scent of blood she dripped all over the tree. They're Luke's problem now. She hopes they tear him apart. Hopefully, Bear will run away. The dog doesn't deserve to die. It's not his fault his human is a monster.

Blood still seeps slowly through the wrappings on her foot.

She tries to ignore the excruciating pain.

The air around her naked body cools rapidly. She accepts it won't be long though. Tonight, she doesn't have anything to help hold her to the tree when she falls asleep.

Fear and peace war within her in equal measure. She's ready for the nightmare to be over. Her only consolation is that the game was rigged. By choosing her fate, she leaves him with "clean" hands.

For hours after dark has fallen, she remains awake. Her will to survive is stronger than her despair. Eventually, she nods off. The first time she does, she begins to lose her balance and jerks back awake.

The night has thankfully hidden the distance between her and the forest floor.

She repositions herself sideways across several branches and closes her eyes again. Her naked body shivers. The air up here is colder than it had been below where she was sheltered from the wind.

She drifts off.

Her body rolls in her sleep.

The thin branches bend.

Something snaps.

The sound wakes her.

She's moving, away from the tree trunk, steadily downward.

Her hands reach out to grasp and stop her fall, but she has no strength left. The thin, soft pine needles slip through her grasp.

Then she's falling. The soft ends of branches slap her tired, abused body.

Suddenly, all is black.

13

Author's Notes

Well, that was a wild ride. But buckle up. They only get crazier from here.

When I first started writing His Game, I planned to make them a series of novellas. Apparently, my brain doesn't like working in short formats that much because the next one is way longer. And spicier.

Fun facts:

Seven Nights in Barcelona is not a real movie. At least I couldn't find anything on Google when I made up a film for Sandra to go see.

I'm not a huge fan of romance books or movies.

I haven't read or watched *The Notebook.*

I started writing this story by hand in a notebook. Halfway through I got tired of how much slower that was than typing. (Plus, you have to type it up after you write it.)

I stumbled through the romance part of this book and had to talk a LOT of that part out with my husband. I'm hoping that you'll find my romance skills much improved in the next His Game.

* * *

Now I know that some of what Luke says doesn't add up if you read the prequel His Game: The First Time. Just like his story about why he's living out in the woods, he makes up shit to tell his victims. When doing edits, I decided to not change what he tells Sandra about his first *game.* But I also don't think he considers his first victim to be his first game. So I'm probably going to write that at some point too.

I had several people ask me for more from Luke's (John's) point of view. This got me thinking about my plans for season three, His Game: Riviera Maya, and I think I'm going to write that season with dual points of view. I'm really looking forward to that.

Thank you so much for reading! I appreciate each and every one of my readers.

You can subscribe to my newsletter here: TirzahMMHawkins.com.

* * *

My Ream subscribers get early access to everything I write. And even if you don't want to subscribe, you can sample the first three episodes of every serial story published there for free. ReamStories.com/TirzahMMHawkins.

His Game: Suburbia (Teaser)

Thanks for reading His Game: The Woods. Where one game ends, another begins. Please enjoy this opening sneak preview of His Game: Suburbia.

* * *

"Send a topless photo to this number within an hour or Kari will lose a fingernail. Contact the police or tell anyone, and Kari will lose a finger."

"What the hell? What kind of sick joke is this?" Jenn stands in the home office holding a white sheet of copy paper. Moments ago, she'd been watching Netflix while eating a sandwich when she heard the printer in the other room turn on and start spitting something out. Her heart instantly raced at the sound. She's the only one home and hadn't told it to do anything.

And this isn't the first time it's happened.

Jenn checks the time. Her roommate, Kari, should be getting off work soon and would usually be home within the half-hour.

Jenn's next thought is to call Kari and make sure she's okay before she crumples the spiteful thing up and throws it in the trash. She pulls out her phone and hits the icon to call her roommate from the top of her favorites list. It rings and goes to voicemail.

"Fuck. Hey, Kar, call me back when you get this. Something

happened again, and I need to know that you are all right."

Jenn hits the end button, pulls up the text thread with her roommate, and types out, "Call me back now. Please."

She locks her phone and stands there staring at the paper. The words on it tease her and twist her stomach into knots. *This can't be real.* She would have easily dismissed it as a prank except, *Why is Kari's name on here?* She'd assumed that the person who'd hacked into their printer the first time was a stranger, but this signals it could be someone they know. Who do they know that would be this sadistic?

Jenn sets the paper down on her desk and redials Kari. Voice-mail.

Not again!

"Kari, this is an emergency. You need to call me back NOW!" She sends the same words in another text.

Why do they want a topless photo of me? And how are they getting access to our printer? Again? We just changed the wifi password.

Jenn takes the paper back out to the living room where she has room to pace. The screensaver on the smart TV bounces around. The sight of her lunch sitting there on the end table makes her nauseous. She swallows the lump in her throat.

She won't be able to relax or calm down until she knows that Kari is okay. Maybe she isn't off work yet. The two of them are close like sisters and typically tell each other if they will be later than expected.

She'll call me back soon, Jenn tells herself to try to remain calm.

She looks at the phone number on the paper and types it into the text recipient box. "Who is this?" she adds as the message and hits send.

Jenn stares at her phone. Waiting. One of them has to respond.

She glances at the time. 1:30 pm. Does that mean the time

runs out at 2 or 2:30? Either way, she'd feel a lot better if she heard from Kari before then.

Minutes tick by. Jenn can't stop looking at her phone or sit down. She walks back and forth in the living room with her phone in hand or leans up against a counter in the kitchen staring at it, commanding it in her mind to notify her about Kari.

The first possible deadline comes and goes without a response from Kari or the number on the page. A lump forms in her throat. Her stomach hurts from the tension.

The final deadline passes. Jenn hasn't received any calls or texts in the past hour. Kari should have been home by now.

When the phone rings, Jenn jerks and emits a startled cry. The caller identification reads St. Vincent Medical Center. Praying the worst hasn't happened, Jenn hits the green answer button. "Hello."

"Yes, I'm looking for Jennifer Creed."

"That's me!"

"We're calling about Kari Wayde."

"Yes! Is she okay?"

"Kari's a bit shaken and has sustained minor injuries."

"Oh my God. I'll be right there." Jenn grabs her purse and keys and runs out the door.

* * *

Well, I hope you enjoyed that teaser. Don't forget, you can read everything before it's released by subscribing at Ream-Stories.com/TirzahMMHawkins.

About the Author

Tirzah M.M. Hawkins is an author of all things dark including horror, fantasy, and snippets of sci-fi. She began writing stories when she was ten years old. Some of her favorites reads at that age were The Hobbit and The Chronicles of Narnia.

Her older brother handed her Stephen King's Eyes of the Dragon when she was twelve, and she hasn't stopped reading his books since. Her other favorite King books are The Talisman, Cell, Cycle of the Werewolf, IT, The Stand, and she could go on and on and on.

After watching too many horror movies at a young age, she has only recently been able to start sleeping with her feet uncovered at night.

She lives with her husband, Daniel, and their many fur (and feathered) babies including at any given time dogs, cats, horses, goats, pigs (that have happy lives until they are eaten), and chickens (who are only around for eggs).

Her favorite hobbies are reading, writing, researching, singing, and listening to music.

When you sign up for her newsletter, you can be the first to learn about her new works as well receive reading recommendations of stories that she has enjoyed.

Sign up here: TirzahMMHawkins.com

You can connect with me on:

https://linktr.ee/tirzahmmhawkins

https://www.facebook.com/groups/tirzahmmhawkins

Also by Tirzah M.M. Hawkins

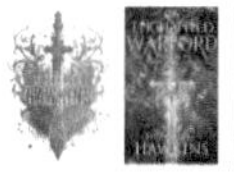

The Party is on Ream!!

If you've ever wanted to hang out and chat with an author about their stories, then you definitely need to join my Ream subscription. Why is it so great? I'm glad you asked.

Ream is where I host my private community for my fans. Feel free to follow me and just consume the free stuff which includes reviews of the books I read and certain free stories.

Or dive on in and sign up for a book box-level subscription. Every quarter, I send out a book box filled with signed books, fun items that I picked out or had made for you, and an item that I made or painted. That last thing used to be a paint pour, but I'm branching out into resin and other fun things.

You and I can dive deeper into my stories on Ream. Readers can leave comments on individual paragraphs as they read. I'll read those and respond when I have something to say back.

Want to dip your toe in? I made a custom code for you. ONEFREE

Enter that code when you sign up to get your first month as a Citizen or Courtier in my Ream realm for free. How does it get better than that?

I don't know, but it will. Especially if we keep asking.

I hope to see you on Ream. Find the link for it here: TirzahMMHawkins.com.

If you aren't interested in my subscription, then you can still find the links to everything that I've written and published at TirzahMMHawkins.com. That's the hub to find everything that I would like you to find.

The Monarch's Daughter

A child in trouble. An unlikely hero. A universe in distress.

In a galaxy abandoned by elves, only one remains: a cruel and unforgiving leader seeking to control his living experiments.

Meanwhile, a young girl's world is torn asunder by a man unwittingly thrown into her life after destroying everything she's ever cared about.

Join Flynae's journey as she struggles for freedom she may never achieve while falling for the warlord who murdered her father.

Will she break free from her sadistic tormentors, and realize her destiny?

Trusting the Enemy, the first book in The Monarch's Daughter, is a sci-fi-fueled, epic fantasy following an emerging heroine with an unexpected and taboo love interest. If you love His Dark Materials and Game of Thrones, then you'll love The Monarch's Daughter.

Excerpt:

"Flynae, wait here." Issiah, her father, forcefully nudges her toward a doorway. Something in his voice compels her to obey. Worry creases his forehead and narrows his eyes as he kneels to be on a similar level with her. Warm hands pull her hood up over her head and caress her face.

A deep dread creeps over her, leaving her skin prickling in its wake. She swallows hard and glances from his bright emerald feline eyes, the same shade and shape as hers, to the street ahead of them.

This part of the city holds the old-world charm of ages

almost forgotten from long ago, a stark contrast to the modern skyscrapers and architecture just a couple miles away. The brick and wooden houses lining the cobblestone streets sit a wide enough distance apart to welcome pedestrians, but near enough to each other to deter all but single-rider vehicles to enter, leaving the alleyway a pleasant, welcoming place for those on foot to escape the noisy bustle of the capital.

Today, a shadow casts icy fingers over the normally warm and inviting area. Ripples from an advancing darkness issue forth and hit her body like violent shockwaves.

Her breath quickens. With the gift and curse of an inhuman wisdom beyond her short four years, she recognizes something is different.

For several months, she's walked these streets twice a week with her father, without incident, to dance lessons. Despite fighting to keep calm, panic grips her chest with an iron fist. Since her birthday three months ago, her gift of sight keeps growing, the images and premonitions becoming clearer and more frequent.

"Peace, Flynae," Issiah whispers a Kaliah boon to her. "All will be well." The corners of his lips turn up, softening his face in a painfully beautiful way.

She smiles, tremulously in response, though tears well in her eyes. One spills down her cheek.

He wipes away the rogue drop. "No crying in front of humans, my daughter." His voice is kind yet stern.

She nods and rubs the extra moisture from her face. His eyes shine his approval. A tightness twists her gut.

This is goodbye.

While her father might not understand the depth of the situation, her sight whispers an undeniable premonition. And lately, her premonitions, good or bad, come true.

Flynae lowers her head and closes her eyes asking in their kind's tradition for a blessing. Her father places his hands on either side of her head and kisses her forehead.

She inhales his scent, burning it into her memory. Though her whole body trembles, she tells herself he must know what is best. Huddling back into the doorway, she hides in the shadows as best she can.

The distance between them widens to a chasm as he leaves her. He walks down the street. Before he's out of sight, he stops and waits.

This isn't right. She looks down at her hands which were just moments ago disguised to appear human by her father's energy. The protection is now tenuous. Her fingertips flash back and forth in front of her from short, manicured nails to long, sharp Kaliah claws.

Knowing she must be quiet, she stifles a cry. Her father's abilities have never failed no matter how far apart they were.

As if he sensed her increasing alarm, his gaze turns back toward her. His mouth pressed together in a flat line, his features showing distress and hesitancy for the first time.

He isn't well.

***

Don't stop reading now. Sample the first three chapters for free: ReamStories.com/TirzahMMHawkins

Dark: A Creature Survival Horror Series
An ongoing survival struggle series. Overnight, most of the human population is wiped out by creatures that survive in the dark. Don't turn out your lights.

Come along for a wild ride in this creepy, apocalyptic, survival, horror story.

Excerpt:

All it takes is a shadow. They can't come into the light. Any light. But that hasn't stopped them from wiping out most of mankind.

There were thirty-seven in the group when Courtney and I found Willis's group, making them thirty-nine.

Willis found us rather. Matt was driving a truck through our neighborhood that morning. Willis was standing in the bed calling out on a bullhorn for survivors.

At first, I couldn't convince myself that the voice we heard was real. I hadn't heard another human voice besides Courtney's in six days, and Courtney was scarcely talking then. It only took me a moment to know that I would rather risk falling into the hands of humans, no matter their intentions, than spend the rest of my nights in that bathroom.

Courtney had refused to leave the bathroom since that first night when they came and killed our parents. We slept during the day as much as we could because we spent the nights bracing the door against them.

They always came back at night. Every night, without fail. From the sound of it on that last night, there had been more of them. I suspected that we were the last of the nearby prey. They were getting hungry. It was only a matter of time before they would find some way to get to Courtney and me. I had to do something.

The power had given out two days before. We spent our nights in the glow of a camping lantern. I was sitting there sharing the last packet of toaster pastries with Courtney when I heard the voice.

"Is anyone there? We have safety."

We have safety. The words pulled at my being even as my brain told me not to trust them. *Don't get your hopes up.* When you're fifteen, and something they can't describe in your high school biology book comes into your house at night and kills your parents as they sleep, you wonder if safety is a real thing.

"Is anyone alive? Please come out. We can help you."

I look at Courtney, pleading with my eyes to be okay with meeting others. For the past week, she hasn't for one moment stopped looking like an injured baby deer.

Courtney violently shakes her head "no" and leaves me in indecision agony.

We can't stay here though. I know that. Any night now could be the night that there are too many of them for us to hold back. The bathroom door is thin; and last night, in the middle of our nightly struggles, I heard it crack. The sound sent chills down my spine in spite of the sweat that fell from my forehead.

These people could be the answer to my prayers. I had decided to drag Courtney from the bathroom today in search of a safer place to hunker down at night. If only we knew someone with a bomb shelter or something similar. I won't let these creatures tear Courtney apart the way they did our parents.

I can still picture it all so clearly.

***

Don't stop reading now. Sample the first three chapters for

free: <u>ReamStories.com/TirzahMMHawkins</u>